His Forbidden Fruit.
His Ultimate Temptation.

The woman whose very existence had been like a corrosive acid coursing through his arteries. The woman he would have been eternally grateful if he never saw again till the day he died. He would have given anything to wake up one day free of her memory.

And it was her who'd woken up free of his.

The red-hot fist that had been squeezing his heart since he'd hurtled to the crash site to find her lying inert almost drove its tentacles inside his heart.

She was telling him she didn't remember the existence that was the bane of his. She'd forgotten the very identity that had been behind the destruction of one life. And the poisoning of his own.

And he shouldn't care. Shouldn't *have* cared.

But he did.

Dear Reader,

It was such a thrill for me to write my first surgeon hero for Silhouette Desire.

I've written doctors before, but while in my other books medicine itself played a big part in the story, in this one I wanted to concentrate on and demonstrate in full measure why a surgeon can be such an irresistibly romantic hero.

So I created Rodrigo Valderrama, the epitome of that hero. He is not only a self-made and phenomenal success, he is a savior, a protector. A tower of strength with extraordinary skills and knowledge, a man to lean on, whose strength of mind and will is surpassed only by that of his passion and tenderness. And in taking care of the injured as well as amnesic and pregnant Cybele Wilkinson, he goes all out demonstrating those qualities that are everything a woman can dream of.

I loved writing Rodrigo so much, and the passionate, deeply emotional relationship that develops between him and Cybele, that I hope I will be writing more surgeons in the future.

I also hope that reading their story will give you as much pleasure as writing it gave me.

I would love to hear from you at oliviagates@gmail.com. You can also visit me on the Web at www.oliviagates.com.

Enjoy, and thanks for reading.

Olivia Gates

OLIVIA GATES

BILLIONAIRE, M.D.

Silhouette® Desire

Published by Silhouette Books

America's Publisher of Contemporary Romance

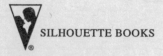 **SILHOUETTE BOOKS**

ISBN-13: 978-0-373-73018-6

BILLIONAIRE, M.D.

Recycling programs
for this product may
not exist in your area.

Books by Olivia Gates

Silhouette Desire

The Desert Lord's Baby #1872
The Desert Lord's Bride #1884
The Desert King #1896
†*The Once and Future Prince* #1942
†*The Prodigal Prince's Seduction* #1948
†*The Illegitimate King* #1954
Billionaire, M.D. #2005

*Throne of Judar
†The Castaldini Crown

OLIVIA GATES

has always pursued creative passions—singing and many handicrafts. She still does, but only one of her passions grew gratifying enough, consuming enough, to become an ongoing career. Writing.

She is most fulfilled when she is creating worlds and conflicts for her characters, then exploring and untangling them bit by bit, sharing her protagonists' every heart-wrenching heartache and hope, their every heart-pounding doubt and trial, until she leads them to an indisputably earned and gloriously satisfying happy ending.

When she's not writing, she is a doctor, a wife to her own alpha male and a mother to one brilliant girl and one demanding Angora cat. Visit Olivia at www.oliviagates.com.

To Natashya and Shane.
This one is definitely for you both.

One

She opened her eyes to another world.

A world filled with grainy grayness, like a TV channel with no transmission. But she didn't care.

This world had an angel watching over her.

And not just any angel. An archangel. If archangels were the personification of beauty and power, were hewn out of living rock and bronze and unadulterated maleness.

His image floated in the jumble of light and shadow, making her wonder if this was a dream. Or a hallucination. Or worse.

Probably worse. In spite of the angel's presence. Or because of it. Angels didn't watch over anyone who wasn't in some serious trouble, did they?

Would be a shame if he turned out to be the angel of death. Why make him so breathtaking if he was just a life-force extractor? He was way overqualified. Such overkill was uncalled for, if you asked her. Or maybe his extreme attractiveness was designed to make his targets willing to go where he led?

She'd be more than willing. *If* she could move.

She couldn't. Gravity overwhelmed her, squashed her back onto something that suddenly felt like a bed of thorns. Every cell in her body started to squirm, every nerve firing impulses. But the cells had no connection to each other and the nerves were unable to muster one spark of voluntary movement. Distress bombarded her, noise rose in her ears, pounding, nauseating her....

His face came closer, stilled the vertigo, swept over the cacophony, stifling it.

Her turmoil subsided. She didn't have to fight the pull of gravity, didn't have to fear the paralysis.

He was here. And he'd take care of everything.

She had no idea how she knew that. But she knew it.

She knew *him*.

Not that she had any idea who he was.

But everything inside her told her that she was safe, that everything would be okay. Because he was here.

Now if only she could get any part of her to work.

She shouldn't feel so inert upon waking up. But was she waking up? Or was she dreaming? That would explain the detachment between brain and body. That would explain *him*. He was too much to be real.

But she knew he was real. She just knew she wasn't imaginative enough to have made him up.

She knew something else, too. This man was important. In general. And to her, he was more than important. Vital.

"Cybele?"

Was that his voice? That dark, fathomless caress?

It so suited the sheer magnificence of his face....

"Can you hear me?"

Boy, could she. She more than heard him. His voice spread across her skin, her pores soaking it up as if they were starved for nourishment. It permeated her with its richness, its every inflection sparking an inert nerve, restarting a vital process, reviving her.

"Cybele, if you can hear me, if you're awake this time, *por favor*, answer me."

Por favor? Spanish? Figured. So that's where the tinge of an accent came from—English intertwining with the sensuous music of the Latin tongue. She wanted to answer him. She wanted him to keep talking. Each syllable out of those works of art he had for lips, crooned in that intoxicating voice, was lulling her back to oblivion, this time a blissful one.

His face filled her field of vision. She could see every shard of gold among the emerald, moss and caramel that swirled into a luminous color she was certain she'd never seen except in his eyes.

She wanted to stab her fingers into the lushness of his raven mane, cup that leonine head, bring him even closer so she could pore over every strand's hue and radiance. She wanted to trace each groove and slash and plane that painted his face in complexity, wanted to touch each radiation of character.

This was a face mapped with anxiety and responsibility and distinction. She wanted to absorb the first, ease the second and marvel at the third. She wanted those lips against her own, mastering, filling her with the tongue that wrapped around those words and created such magic with them.

She knew she shouldn't be feeling anything like that now, that her body wasn't up to her desires. Her *body* knew that, but didn't acknowledge its incapacitation. It just needed him, close, all that maleness and bulk and power, all that tenderness and protection.

She craved this man. She'd always craved him.

"Cybele, *por Dios*, say something."

It was the raggedness, tearing at the power of his voice, that stirred her out of her hypnosis, forced her vocal cords to tauten, propelled air out of her lungs through them to produce the sound he demanded so anxiously.

"I c-can hear you…."

That came out an almost soundless rasp. From the way he tilted his ear toward her mouth, it was clear he wasn't sure whether she *had* produced sound or if he'd imagined it, whether it had been words or just a groan.

She tried again. "I'm a-awake…I think…I hope, a-and I h-hope you're r-real…."

She couldn't say anything more. Fire lanced in her throat, sealing it with a molten agony. She tried to cough up what felt like red-hot steel splinters before they burned through her larynx. Her sand-filled eyes gushed tears, ameliorating their burning dryness.

"Cybele!"

And he was all around her. He raised her, cradled her in the curve of a barricade of heat and support, seeping warmth into her frozen, quivering bones. She sank in his power, surrendered in relief as he cupped her head.

"Don't try to talk anymore. You were intubated for long hours during your surgery and your larynx must be sore."

Something cool touched her lips, then something warm and spicily fragrant lapped at their parched seam. Not his lips or his tongue. A glass and a liquid. She instinctively parted her lips and the contents rushed in a gentle flow, filling her mouth.

When she didn't swallow, he angled her head more securely. "It's a brew of anise and sage. It will soothe your throat."

He'd anticipated her discomfort, had been ready with a remedy. But why was he explaining? She would swallow anything he gave her. If she could without feeling as if nails were being driven into her throat. But he wanted her to. She had to do what he wanted.

She squeezed her eyes against the pain, swallowed. The liquid slid through the rawness, its peppery tinge bringing more tears to her eyes. That lasted only seconds. The soreness subsided under the balmy taste and temperature.

She moaned with relief, feeling rejuvenated with every encouraging sweep of tenderness that his thumb brushed over her cheek as she finished the rest of the glass's contents.

"Better now?"

The solicitude in his voice, in his eyes, thundered through her. She shuddered under the impact of her gratitude, her need to hide inside him, dissolve in his care. She tried to answer him, but this time it was emotion that clogged her throat.

But she *had* to express her thankfulness.

His face was so close, clenched with concern, more magnificent in proximity, a study of perfection in slashes of strength and carvings of character. But haggardness had sunk redness into his eyes, iron into his jaw, and the unkemptness of a few days' growth of rough silk over that jaw and above those lips caused her heart to twist. The need to absorb his discomforts and worries as he had hers mushroomed inside her.

She turned her face, buried her lips into his hewn cheek. The bristle of his beard, the texture of his skin, the taste and scent of him tingled on her flesh, soaked into her senses. A gust of freshness and virility coursed through her, filled her lungs. His breath, rushing out on a ragged exhalation.

She opened her lips for more just as he jerked around to face her. It brought his lips brushing hers. And she knew.

This was the one thing she'd needed. This intimacy. With him.

Something she'd always had before and had missed?

Something she'd had before and had lost? Something she'd never had and had long craved?

It didn't matter. She had it now.

She glided her lips against his, the flood of sensuality and sweetness of her flesh sweeping against his sizzling through her.

Then her lips were cold and bereft, the enclosure of muscle and maleness around her gone.

She slumped against what she now realized was a bed.

Where had he gone? Had it all been a hallucination? A side effect of emerging from a coma?

Her eyes teared up again with the loss. She turned her swimming head, searching for him, terrified she'd find only emptiness.

Far from emptiness, she registered her surroundings for the first time, the most luxurious and spacious hospital suite she'd ever seen. But if he wasn't there...

Her darting gaze and hurtling thoughts came to an abrupt halt.

He *was* there. Standing where he'd been when she'd first opened her eyes. But his image was distorted this time, turning him from an angel into a wrathful, inapproachable god who glowered down at her with disapproval.

She blinked once, then again, her heart shedding its sluggish rhythm for frantic pounding.

It was no use. His face remained cast in coldness. Instead of the angel she'd thought would do anything to protect her, this was the face of a man who'd stand aside and brood down at her as she drowned.

She stared up at him, something that felt as familiar as a second skin settling about her. Despondence.

It had been an illusion. Whatever she'd thought she'd seen

on his face, whatever she'd felt flooding her in waves, had been her disorientation inventing what she wanted to see, to feel.

"It's clear you can move your head. Can you move everything else? Are you in any pain? Blink if it's too uncomfortable to talk. Once for yes, twice for no."

Tears surged into her eyes again. She blinked erratically. A low rumble unfurled from his depths. Must be frustration with her inability to follow such a simple direction.

But she couldn't help it. She now recognized his questions for what they were. Those asked of anyone whose consciousness had been compromised, as she was now certain hers had been. Ascertaining level of awareness, then sensory and motor functions, then pain level and site. But there was no personal worry behind the questions anymore, just clinical detachment.

She could barely breathe with missing his tenderness and anxiety for her well-being. Even if she'd imagined them.

"Cybele! Keep your eyes open, stay with me."

The urgency in his voice snapped through her, made her struggle to obey him. "I c-can't…."

He seemed to grow bigger, his hewn face etched with fierceness, frustration rippling off him. Then he exhaled. "Then just answer my questions, and I'll leave you to rest."

"I f-feel numb but…" She concentrated, sent signals to her toes. They wiggled. That meant everything in between them and her brain was in working order. "Seems…motor functions are…intact. Pain—not certain. I feel sore…like I've been flattened under a—a brick wall. B-but i-it's not pain indicating damage…"

Just as the last word was out, all aches seemed to seep from every inch of her body to coalesce in one area. Her left arm.

In seconds she shot beyond the threshold of containable pain into brain-shredding agony.

It spilled from her lips on a butchered keen. "M-my arm…"

She could swear he didn't move. But she found him beside her again, as if by magic, and cool relief splashed over the hot skewers of pain, putting them out.

She whimpered, realized what he'd done. She had an intravenous line in her right arm. He'd injected a drug—a narcotic analgesic from the instantaneous action—into the saline, flicked the drip to maximum.

"Are you still in pain?" She shook her head. He exhaled heavily. "That's good enough for now. I'll come back later…." He started to move away.

"No." Her good hand shot out without conscious volition, fueled by the dread that he'd disappear and she'd never see him again. This felt instinctive, engrained, the desperation that she could lose him. Or was it the resignation that he was already lost to her?

Her hand tightened around his, as if stronger contact would let her read his mind, reanimate hers, remind her what he'd been to her.

He relinquished her gaze, his incandescent one sweeping downward to where her hand was gripping his. "Your reflexes, motor power and coordination seem to be back to normal. All very good signs you're recovering better than my expectations."

From the way he said that, she guessed his expectations had ranged from pessimistic to dismal. "That…should be…a relief."

"Should be? You're not glad you're okay?"

"I am. I guess. Seems…I'm not…all there yet." The one thing that made her feel anything definite was him. And he could have been a mile away with the distance he'd placed between them. "So…what happened…to me?"

The hand beneath hers lurched. "You don't remember?"

"It's all a…a blank."

His own gaze went blank for an endless moment. Then it gradually focused on her face, until she felt it was penetrating her, like an X-ray that would let him scan her, decipher her condition.

"You're probably suffering from post-traumatic amnesia. It's common to forget the traumatic episode."

Spoken like a doctor. Everything he'd said and done so far had pointed to him being one.

Was that all he was to her? Her doctor? Was that how he knew her? He'd been her doctor before the "traumatic episode" and she'd had a crush on him? Or had he just read the vital statistics on her admission papers? Had she formed dependence on and fascination for him when she'd been drifting in and out of consciousness as he'd managed her condition? Had she kissed a man who was here only in his professional capacity? A man who could be in a relationship, maybe married with children?

The pain of her suppositions grew unbearable. And she just had to know. "Wh-who are you?"

The hand beneath hers went still. All of him seemed to become rock, as if her question had a Medusa effect.

When he finally spoke, his voice had dipped an octave lower, a bass, slowed-down rasp, "You don't know me?"

"Sh-should I?" She squeezed her eyes shut as soon as the words were out. She'd just kissed him. And she was telling him that she had no idea who he was. "I know I should…b-but I can't r-remember."

Another protracted moment. Then he muttered, "You've forgotten me?"

She gaped up at him, shook her head, as if the movement would slot some comprehension into her mind. "Uh…I may have forgotten…how to speak, too. I had this…distinct belief language skills…are the last to go…e-even in total…memory loss. I thought…saying I can't remember you…was the same as saying…I forgot who y-you are."

His gaze lengthened until she thought he wouldn't speak again. Ever. Then he let out a lung-deflating exhalation, raked his fingers through his gleaming wealth of hair. "I'm the one who's finding it hard to articulate. Your language skills are in perfect condition. In fact, I've never heard you speak that much in one breath."

"M-many fractured…breaths…you mean."

He nodded, noting her difficulty, then shook his head, in wonder it seemed. "One word to one short sentence at a time was your norm."

"So you…*do* know me. E-extensively, it seems."

The wings of his thick eyebrows drew closer together. "I wouldn't label my knowledge of you extensive."

"I'd label it…en-encyclopedic."

Another interminable silence. Then another darkest-bass murmur poured from him, thrumming every neuron in her hypersensitive nervous system. "It seems your memory deficit is the only thing that's extensive here, Cybele."

She knew she should be alarmed at this verdict. She wasn't.

She sighed. "I love…the way…you say…my name."

And if she'd thought he'd frozen before, it was nothing compared to the stillness that snared him now. It was as if time and space had hit a pause button and caught him in their stasis field.

Then, in such a controlled move, as if he were afraid she was made of soap bubbles and she'd burst if he as much as rattled the air around her, he sat down beside her on her pristine white bed.

His weight dipped the mattress, rolling her slightly toward

him. The side of her thigh touched his through the thickness of his denim pants, through her own layers of covering. Something slid through the mass of aches that constituted her body, originating from somewhere deep within her, uncoiling through her gut to pool into her loins.

She was barely functioning, and he could wrench that kind of response from her every depleted cell? What would he do to her if she were in top condition? What *had* he done? Because she was certain this response to him wasn't new.

"You really don't remember who I am at all."

"You really…are finding it hard…to get my words, aren't you?" Her lips tugged. She was sure there was no humor in this situation, that when it all sank in she'd be horrified about her memory loss and what it might signify of neurological damage.

But for now, she just found it so endearing that this man, who she didn't need memory to know was a powerhouse, was so shaken by the realization.

It also said he cared what happened to her, right? She could enjoy that belief now, even if it proved to be a delusion later.

She sighed again. "I thought it was clear…what I meant. At least it sounded…clear to me. But what would I know? When I called your…knowledge of me…encyclopedic, I should have added…compared to mine. I haven't only…forgotten who you are, I have no idea…who *I* am."

Two

Rodrigo adjusted the drip, looking anywhere but at Cybele.

Cybele. His forbidden fruit. His ultimate temptation.

The woman whose very existence had been like corrosive acid coursing through his arteries. The woman the memory of whom he would have given anything to wake up free of one day.

And it was she who'd woken up free of the memory of him.

It had been two days since she'd dropped this bomb on him.

He was still reverberating with the shock.

She'd told him she didn't remember the existence that was the bane of his. She'd forgotten the very identity that had been behind the destruction of one life. And the poisoning of his own.

And he shouldn't care. Shouldn't *have* cared. Not beyond

the care he offered his other patients. By all testimonies, he went above and beyond the demands of duty and the dictates of compassion for each one. He shouldn't have neglected everyone and everything to remain by her side, to do everything for her when he could have delegated her care to the highly qualified professionals he'd painstakingly picked and trained, those he paid far more than money to keep doing the stellar job they did.

He hadn't. During the three interminable days after her surgery until she woke up, whenever he'd told himself to tend to his other duties, he couldn't. She'd been in danger, and it had been beyond him to leave her.

Her inert form, her closed eyes, had been what had ruled him. The drive to get her to move, to open her eyes and look at him with those endless inky skies that had been as inescapable as a black hole since they'd first had him in their focus, had been what motivated him.

Periodically she had opened them, but there had been no sight or comprehension in them, no trace of the woman who'd invaded and occupied his thoughts ever since he'd laid eyes on her.

Yet he'd prayed that, if she never came back, her body would keep on functioning, that she'd keep opening her eyes, even if it was just a mechanical movement with no sentience behind it.

Two days ago, she'd opened those eyes and the blankness had been replaced by the fog of confusion. His heart had nearly torn a hole in his ribs when coherence had dawned in her gaze. Then she'd looked at him and there had been more.

He should have known then that she was suffering from something he hadn't factored in. Finding her distance and disdain replaced by warmth that had escalated to heat should have given him his first clue. Having her nuzzle him like a feline delighted at finding her owner, then that kiss that had rocked him to his foundations, should have clenched the diagnosis.

The Cybele Wilkinson he knew—his nemesis—would never have looked at or touched him that way if she were in her right mind. If she knew who he was.

It had still taken her saying that she wasn't and didn't to explain it all. And he'd thought *that* had explained it all.

But it was even worse. She didn't remember herself.

There was still something far worse. The temptation not to fill in the spaces that had consumed her memories, left her mind a blank slate. A slate that could be inscribed with anything that didn't mean they had to stay enemies.

But they had to. Now more than ever.

"I see you're still not talking to me."

Her voice, no longer raspy, but a smooth, rich, molten caress sweeping him from the inside out, forced him to turn his eyes to her against his will. "I've talked to you every time I came in."

"Yeah, two sentences every two hours for the past two days." She huffed something that bordered on amusement. "Feels like part of your medication regimen. Though the sparseness really contrasts with the intensiveness of your periodic checkups."

He could have relegated *those*, which hadn't needed to be so frequent, or so thorough, to nurses under his residents' supervision. But he hadn't let anyone come near her.

He turned his eyes away again, pretended to study her chart. "I've been giving you time to rest, for your throat to heal and for you to process the discovery of your amnesia."

She fidgeted, dragging his gaze back to her. "My throat has been perfectly fine since yesterday. It's a miracle what some soothing foods and drinks and talking to oneself can do. And I haven't given my amnesia any thought. I know I should be alarmed, but I'm not. Maybe it's a side effect of the trauma, and it will crash on me later as I get better. *Or*…I'm subconsciously relieved not to remember."

His voice sounded alien as he pushed an answer past the brutal temptation, the guilt, the rage, at her, at himself, at the whole damned universe. "Why wouldn't you want to remember?"

Her lips crooked. "If I knew, it wouldn't be a subconscious wish, would it? Am I still making sense only in my own ears?"

He tore his gaze away from her lips, focused on her eyes, cleared thorns from his throat. "No. I am not having an easy time processing the fact that you have total memory loss."

"And without memories, my imagination is having a field day thinking of outlandish explanations for why I'm not in a hurry to have my memories back. At least they seem outlandish. They might turn out to be the truth."

"And what are those theories?"

"That I was a notorious criminal or a spy, someone with a dark and dangerous past and who's in desperate need of a second chance, a clean slate. And now that it's been given to me, I'd rather not remember the past—my own identity most of all."

She struggled to sit up, groaning at the aches he knew her body had amassed. He tried to stop himself.

He failed. He lunged to help her, tried not to feel the supple heat of her flesh fill his hands as he pulled her up, adjusted her bed to a gentle slope. He struggled to ignore the gratitude filling her eyes, the softness of trust and willingness exhibited by every inch of her flesh. He roared inwardly at his senses as the feel and scent of her turned his insides to molten lava, his loins to rock. He gritted his teeth, made sure her intravenous line and the other leads monitoring her vital signs were secure.

Her hands joined his in checking her line and leads, an

unconscious action born of engrained knowledge and ongoing application. He stepped away as if from a fiery pit.

She looked up at him, those royal blue eyes filling with a combo of confusion and hurt at his recoil. He took one more step back before he succumbed to the need to erase that crestfallen expression.

She lowered her eyes. "So—you're a doctor. A surgeon?"

He was, for once, grateful for her questions. "Neuro-surgeon."

She raised her eyes again. "And from the medical terms filling my mind and the knowledge of what the machines here are and what the values they're displaying mean—I'm some kind of medical professional, too?"

"You were a senior trauma/reconstructive surgery resident."

"Hmm, that blows my criminal or spy theories out of the water. But maybe I was in another form of trouble before I ended up here? A ruinous malpractice suit? Some catastrophic mistake that killed someone? Was I about to have my medical license revoked?"

"I never suspected you had this fertile an imagination."

"Just trying to figure out why I'm almost relieved I don't remember a thing. Was I perhaps running away to start again where no one knows me? Came here and…hey, where *is* here?"

He almost kept expecting her to say *gotcha*. But the notion of Cybele playing a trick on him was more inconceivable than her total memory loss. "This is my private medical center. It's on the outskirts of Barcelona."

"We're in Spain?" Her eyes widened. His heart kicked. Even with her lids still swollen and her face bruised and pallid, she was the most beautiful thing he'd ever seen. "Okay, scratch that question. As far as my general knowledge can tell—and I feel it remains unaffected—there is no Barcelona anywhere else."

"Not that I know of, no."

"So—I sound American."

"You are American."

"And you're Spanish?"

"Maybe to the world, which considers all of Spain one community and everyone who hails from there as Spanish. But I am Catalan. And though in Catalonia we have the same king, and a constitution that declares 'the indissoluble unity of the Spanish nation,' we were the first to be recognized as a *Nacionalidad* and a *Comunidad Autónoma* or a distinct historical nationality and an autonomous community, along with the Basque Country and Galicia. There are now seventeen such communities that make up Spain, with our rights to self-government recognized by the constitution."

"Fascinating. Sort of a federation, like the United States."

"There are similarities, but it's a different system. The regional governments are responsible for education, health, social services, culture, urban and rural development and, in some places, policing. But contrary to the States, Spain is described as a decentralized country, with central government spending estimated at less than twenty percent." And he was damned if he knew why he was telling her all that, now of all times.

She chewed her lower lip that was once again the color of deep pink rose petals. His lips tingled with the memory of those lips, plucking at them, bathing them with intoxicating heat and moistness. "I knew some of that, but not as clearly as you've put it."

He exhaled his aggravation at the disintegration of his sense and self-control. "Pardon the lesson. My fascination with the differences between the two systems comes from having both citizenships."

"So you acquired the American citizenship?"

"Actually, I was born in the States, and acquired my Spanish citizenship after I earned my medical degree. Long story."

"But you have an accent."

He blinked his surprise at the implication of her words, something he'd never suspected. "I spent my first eight years in an exclusively Spanish-speaking community in the States and learned English only from then on. But I was under the impression I'd totally lost the accent."

"Oh, no, you haven't. And I hope you never lose it. It's *gorgeous*."

Everything inside him surged. This was something else he'd never considered. What she'd do to him if, instead of hostility, admiration and invitation spread on her face, invaded her body, if instead of bristling at the sight of him, she looked at him as if she'd like nothing more than to feast on him. As she was now.

What was going on here? How had memory loss changed her character and attitude so diametrically? Did that point to more neurological damage than he'd feared? Or was this what she was really like, what her reaction to him would have been if not for the events that had messed up their whole situation?

"So…what's your name? What's mine, too, apart from Cybele?"

"You're Cybele Wilkinson. I'm Rodrigo."

"Just…Rodrigo?"

She used to call him Dr. Valderrama, and in situations requiring informality she'd avoided calling him anything at all. But now she pressed back into her pillows, let his name melt on her tongue as if it were the darkest, richest chocolate.

He felt her contented purr cascade down his body, caress his aching hardness….

This was unbelievable. That she could do this to him *now*. Or at all. It was worse than unbelievable. It was unacceptable.

He shredded his response. "Rodrigo Edmundo Arrellano i Bazán Valderrama i de Urquiza."

Her eyes widened a fraction more with each surname. Then a huff that bordered on a giggle escaped her. "I did ask."

His lips twisted. "That's an excerpt of my names, actually. I can rattle off over forty more surnames."

She giggled for real this time. "That's a family tree going back to the Spanish Inquisition."

"The Catalan, and the Spanish in general, take family trees very seriously. Because both maternal and paternal ancestors are mentioned, each name makes such a list. The Catalan also put *i* or *and* between surnames."

"And do I have more than the measly Wilkinson?"

"All I know is that your father's name was Cedric."

"Was? H-he's dead?"

"Since you were six or seven, I believe."

She seemed to have trouble swallowing again. He had to fist his hands against the need to rush to her side again.

His heart still hammered in protest against his restraint when she finally whispered, "Do I have a mother? A family?"

"Your mother remarried and you have four half siblings. Three brothers and one sister. They all live in New York City."

"D-do they know what happened to me?"

"I did inform them. Yesterday." He hadn't even thought of doing so until his head nurse had stressed the necessity of alerting her next of kin. For the seventh time. He hadn't even registered the six previous times she had mentioned it.

He waited for her next logical question. If they were on their way here to claim responsibility for her.

His gut tightened. Even with all he had against her, not the least of which was the reaction she wrenched from him, he hated to have to answer that question. To do so, he'd have to tell her that her family's response to her danger had been so offhand, he'd ended the phone call with her mother on a barked, "Don't bother explaining your situation to me, Mrs. Doherty. I'm sure you'd be of more use at your husband's business dinner than you would be at Cybele's bedside."

But her next question did not follow a logical progression. Just as this whole conversation, which she'd steered, hadn't. "So…what happened to me?"

And this was a question he wanted to avoid as fiercely.

No way to do that now that she'd asked so directly. He exhaled. "You were in a plane crash."

A gasp tore out of her. "I just knew I was in an accident, that I wasn't attacked or anything, but I thought it was an MVA or something. But…a plane crash?" She seemed to struggle with air that had gone thick, lodging in her lungs. He rocked on his heels with the effort not to rush to her with an oxygen mask and soothing hands. "Were there many injured o-or worse?"

Dios. She really remembered nothing. And he was the one who had to tell her. Everything. "It was a small plane. Seated four. There were only…two onboard this time."

"Me and the pilot? I might not remember anything, but I just know I can't fly a plane, small or otherwise."

This was getting worse and worse. He didn't want to answer her. He didn't want to relive the three days before she'd woken up, that had gouged their scars in his psyche and soul.

He could pretend he had a surgery, escape her interrogation.

He couldn't. Escape. Stop himself from answering her. "He was flying the plane, yes."

"Is—is he okay, too?"

Rodrigo gritted his teeth against the blast of pain that detonated behind his sternum. "He's dead."

"Oh, God...." Her tears brimmed again and he couldn't help himself anymore. He closed the distance he'd put between them, stilled the tremors of her hand with both of his. "D-did he die on impact?"

He debated telling her that he had. He could see survivor's guilt mushrooming in her eyes. What purpose did it serve to tell her the truth but make her more miserable?

But then he always told his patients the truth. Sooner or later that always proved the best course of action.

He inhaled. "He died on the table after a six-hour surgery."

During those hours, he'd wrestled with death, gaining an inch to lose two to its macabre pull, knowing that it would win the tug-of-war. But what had wrecked his sanity had been knowing that while he fought this losing battle, Cybele had been lying in his ER tended to by others.

Guilt had eaten through him. Triage had dictated he take care of her first, the one likely to survive. But he couldn't have let Mel go without a fight. It had been an impossible choice. Emotionally, professionally, morally. He'd gone mad thinking she'd die or suffer irreversible damage because he'd made the wrong one.

Then he'd lost the fight for Mel's life among colleagues' proclamations that it had been a miracle he'd even kept him alive for hours when everyone had given up on him at the accident scene.

He'd rushed to her, knowing that while he'd exercised the ultimate futility on Mel, her condition had worsened. Terror of losing her, too, had been the one thing giving him continued access to what everyone extolled as his vast medical knowledge and surgical expertise.

"Tell me, please. The details of his injuries."

He didn't want to tell her how terrible it had all been.

But he had to. He inhaled a stream of what felt like aerosolized acid, then told her.

Her tears flowed steadily over a face gone numb with horror throughout his chilling report.

She finally whispered, "How did the accident happen?"

He needed this conversation to be over. He gritted his teeth. "That is one thing only you can know for sure. And it'll probably be the last memory to return. The crash site and plane were analyzed for possible whys and hows. The plane shows no signs of malfunction and there were no distress transmissions prior to the crash."

"So the pilot just lost control of the plane?"

"It would appear so."

She digested this for a moment. "What about my injuries?"

"You should only concern yourself now with recuperating."

"But I need to know a history of my injuries, their progression and management, to chart my recuperation."

He grudgingly conceded her logic. "On site, you were unconscious. You had a severely bleeding scalp wound and bruising all over your body. But your severest injury was comminuted fractures of your left ulna and radius."

She winced as she looked down on her splinted arm. "What was my Glasgow Coma Scale scoring?"

"Eleven. Best eye response was three, with your eyes opening only in response to speech. Best verbal response was four, with your speech ranging from random words to confused responses.

Best motor function was four with flexion withdrawal response to pain. By the time I operated on you, your GCS had plunged to five."

"Ouch. I was heading for decorticate coma. Did I have intracranial hemorrhage?"

He gave a difficult nod. "It must have been a slow leak. Your initial CTs and MRIs revealed nothing but slight brain edema, accounting for your depressed consciousness. But during the other surgery, I was informed of your deteriorating neurological status, and new tests showed a steadily accumulating subdural hematoma."

"You didn't shave my hair evacuating it."

"No need. I operated via a new minimally invasive technique I've developed."

She gaped at him. "You've developed a new surgical technique? Excuse me while my mind, tattered as it is, barrels in awe."

He grunted something dismissive. She eyed him with a wonder that seemed only to rise at his discomfort. Just as he almost growled *stop it*, she raised one beautifully dense and dark eyebrow at him. "I trust I wasn't the guinea pig for said technique?"

Cybele gazed up at Rodrigo, a smile hovering on her lips.

His own lips tightened. "You're fine, aren't you?"

"If you consider having to get my life story from you as *fine*."

The spectacular wings of his eyebrows snapped together. That wasn't annoyance or affront. That was mortification. Pain, even.

Words couldn't spill fast enough from her battered brain to her lips. "God, that was such a lame joke. Just shows I'm in no condition to know how or when to make one. I owe you my life."

"You owe me nothing. I was doing my job. And I didn't even do it well. I'm responsible for your current condition. It's my failure to manage you first that led to the deepening of the insult to your brai—"

"The pilot's worst injuries were neurological." She cut him short. It physically hurt to see the self-blame eating at him.

"Yes, but that had nothing to do with my decision—"

"And I bet you're the best neurosurgeon on the continent."

"I don't know about that, but being the most qualified one on hand didn't mea—"

"It *did* mean you had to take care of him yourself. And my initial condition misled you into believing my case wasn't urgent. You did the right thing. You fought for this man as he deserved to be fought for. And then you fought for me. And you saved me. And then, I'm certain my condition is temporary."

"We have no way of knowing that. Having total memory loss with the retention of all faculties of language and logic and knowledge and no problem in accumulating new memories is a very atypical form of amnesia. It might never resolve fully."

"Would that be a bad thing, in your opinion? If the idea of regaining my memories is almost…distressing, maybe my life was so bad, I'm better off not remembering it?"

He seemed at a loss for words. Then he finally found some. "I am not in a position to know the answer to that. But I am in a position to know that memory loss is a neurological deficit, and it's my calling to fix those. I can't under any circumstances wish that this wouldn't resolve. Now, if you'll excuse me, I need to tend to my other patients. I'll be back every three hours to check on you."

With a curt nod, he turned and left her, exiting the huge, opulent suite in strides loaded with tense grace.

She wanted to run after him, beg him to come back.

What could possibly explain all this turmoil and her severe attraction to him? Had they been lovers, married even, and they'd separated, or maybe divorced…?

She suddenly lurched as if from the blow of an ax as a memory lodged in her brain. No…a knowledge.

She *was* married.

And it was certainly not to Rodrigo.

Three

Rodrigo did come back in three hours. And stayed for three minutes. Long enough to check on her and adjust her medical management. Then he repeated that pattern for the next three days. She even felt him come in during her fitful sleep.

She hadn't had the chance to tell him what she'd remembered.

No. She hadn't *wanted* to tell him. Discovering she was married, even if she didn't know to whom, wasn't on her list of things to share with him of all people.

And he probably already knew.

She *could* have told him that she'd also remembered who she was. But then, she hadn't remembered much beyond the basics he'd told her.

This boded well for her memory deficit, if it was receding so early.

She didn't want it to recede, wanted to cling to the blankness with all her strength.

But it was no use. A few hours ago, a name had trickled into the parting darkness of her mind. Mel Braddock.

She was certain that was her husband's name. But she couldn't put a face to the name. The only memory she could attach to said name was a profession. General surgeon.

Beyond that, she remembered nothing of the marriage. She knew only that something dark pressed down on her every time the knowledge of it whispered in her mind.

She couldn't possibly feel this way if they'd been on good terms. And if he wasn't here, days after his wife had been involved in a serious accident, were they separated, getting divorced even? She was certain she was still married. Technically, at least. But the marriage was over. That would explain her overriding emotions for Rodrigo, that she innately knew it was okay to feel them.

On the strike of three hours, Rodrigo returned. And she'd progressed from not wanting to bring up any of it to wanting to scream it all at the top of her lungs.

He made no eye contact with her as he strode in flanked by two doctors and a nurse. He never came unescorted anymore. It was as if he didn't want to be alone with her again.

He checked her chart, informed his companions of his adjustment of her medications as if she wasn't in the room much less a medical professional who could understand everything they were saying. Frustration frothed inside her. Then it boiled over.

"I remembered a few things."

Rodrigo went still at her outburst. The other people in the room fidgeted, eyed her uncomfortably before turning uncertain gazes to their boss. Still without looking at her, he hung her chart back at the foot of the bed, murmured something clearly meant for the others' ears alone. They rushed out in a line.

The door had closed behind the last departing figure for over two minutes before he turned his eyes toward her.

She shuddered with the force of his elemental impact.

Oh, please. Let me have the right to feel this way about him.

The intensity of his being buzzed in her bones—of his focus, of his...wariness?

Was he anxious to know what she remembered? Worried about it? Because he suspected what it was—the husband she remembered only in name? He'd told her of her long-dead father, her existing family, but not about that husband. Would he have told her if she hadn't remembered?

But there was something more in his vibe. Something she'd felt before. After she'd kissed him. Disapproval? Antipathy?

Had they been on bad terms before the accident? How could they have been, if she felt this vast attraction to him, untainted by any negativity? Had the falling out been her fault? Was he bitter? Was he now taking care of her to honor his calling, his duty, giving her extra special care for old times' sake, yet unable to resume their intimacy? *Had* they been intimate? Was he her lover?

No. He wasn't.

She might not remember much about herself, but the thought of being in a relationship, no matter how unhealthy, and seeking involvement with another felt abhorrent to her, no matter how inexorable the temptation. And then, there was him. He radiated nobility. She just knew Rodrigo Valderrama would never poach on another man's grounds, never cross the lines of honor, no matter how much he wanted her or how dishonorable the other man was.

But there was one paramount proof that told her they'd never been intimate. Her body. It burned for him but knew it had never had him. It would have borne his mark on its every cell if it had.

So what did it all mean? He had to tell her, before something beside memories short-circuited inside her brain.

He finally spoke. "What did you remember?"

"Who I am. That I'm married." He showed no outward reaction. So he *had* known. "Why didn't you tell me?"

"You didn't ask."

"I asked about family."

"I thought you were asking about flesh-and-blood relatives."

"You're being evasive."

"Am I?" He held her gaze, making her feel he was giving her a psyche and soul scan. Maybe trying to steer her thoughts, too. "So you remember everything?"

She exhaled. "I said I remembered 'a few things.' Seems I'm a stickler for saying exactly what I mean."

"You said you remembered who you were, and your marriage. That's just about everything, isn't it?"

"Not when I remember only the basics about myself, the name you told me, that I went to Harvard Medical School, that I worked at St. Giles Hospital and that I'm twenty-nine. I know far less than the basics about my marriage. I remembered only that I have a husband, and his name and profession."

"That's all?"

"The rest is speculation."

"What kind of speculation?"

"About the absence of both my family and husband more than a week after I've been involved in a major accident. I can only come up with very unfavorable explanations."

"What would those be?"

"That I'm a monster of such megaproportions that no one

felt the need to rush to my bedside." Something flared in his eyes, that harshness. So she was right? He thought so, too? Her heart compressed as she waited for him to confirm or negate her suspicions. When he didn't, she dejectedly had to consider his silence as corroboration, condemnation. She still looked for a way out for herself, for her family. "Unless it is beyond them financially to make the trip here?"

"As far as I know, finances are no issue to your family."

"So you told them I was at death's door, and no one bothered to come."

"I told them no such thing. You weren't at death's door."

"It *could* have gone either way for a while."

Silence. Heavy. Oppressive. Then he simply said, "Yes."

"So I'm on the worst terms with them."

It seemed he'd let this go uncommented on, too. Then he gave a noncommittal shrug. "I don't know about the worst terms. But it's my understanding you're not close."

"Not even with my mother?"

"Especially with your mother."

"Great. See? I was right when I thought I was better off not remembering. Not knowing."

"It isn't as bad as you're painting it. By the time I called your family, you were stable, and there really was nothing for any of them to do but wait like the rest of us. Your mother did call twice for updates, and I told her you were doing very well. Physically. Psychologically, I suggested it might not be a good thing in this early phase for you to be jogged by their presence or contact, any more than you already are."

He was making excuses for her family, her mother. If they'd cared, they wouldn't have been satisfied with long-distance assurances. Or maybe he had discouraged them from coming, so he wouldn't introduce an unpredictable emotional element into her neurological recovery?

The truth was, she didn't care right now how things really stood with her family. What she was barely able to breathe from needing to know was her status with her husband.

"And that's my not-so-bad situation with my family. But from my husband's pointed absence, I can only assume the worst. That maybe we're separated or getting divorced."

She wanted him to say, *Yes, you are*.

Please, say it.

His jaw muscles bunched, his gaze chilled. When he finally spoke it felt like an arctic wind blasting her, freezing her insides with this antipathy that kept spiking out of nowhere.

"Far from being separated, you and your husband have been planning a second honeymoon."

Cybele doubted the plane crashing into the ground had a harder impact than Rodrigo's revelation.

Her mind emptied. Her heart spilled all of its beats at once.

For a long, horrified moment she stared at him, speech skills and thought processes gone, only blind instincts left. They all screamed *run, hide, deny*.

She'd been so certain…so…certain…

"A second honeymoon?" She heard her voice croaking. "Does that mean we…we've been married long?"

He waited an eternity before answering. At least it felt that way. By the time he did, she felt she'd aged ten years. "You were married six months ago."

"Six *months?* And already planning a second honeymoon?"

"Maybe I should have said honeymoon, period. Circumstances stopped you from having one when you first got married."

"And yet my adoring husband isn't here. Our plans probably were an attempt to salvage a marriage that was malfunctioning beyond repair, and we shouldn't have bothered going through the motions…."

She stopped, drenched in mortification. She instinctively knew she wasn't one to spew vindictiveness like that. Her words had been acidic enough to eat through the gleaming marble floor.

Their corrosiveness had evidently splashed Rodrigo. From the way his face slammed shut, he clearly disapproved of her sentiments and the way she'd expressed them. Of her.

"I don't know much about your relationship. But his reason for not being at your bedside *is* uncontestable. He's dead."

She lurched as if he'd backhanded her.

"He was flying the plane," she choked.

"You remember?"

"No. Oh, God." A geyser of nausea shot from her depths. She pitched to the side of the bed. Somehow she found Rodrigo around her, holding her head and a pan. She retched emptily, shook like a bell that had been struck by a giant mallet.

And it wasn't from a blow of grief. It was from one of horror, at the anger and relief that were her instinctive reactions.

What kind of monster was she to feel like that about somebody's death, let alone that of her husband? Even if she'd fiercely wanted out of the relationship. Was it because of what she felt for Rodrigo? She'd wished her husband dead to be with him?

No. *No.* She just knew it hadn't been like that. It had to have been something else. Could her husband have been abusing her? Was she the kind of woman who would have suffered humiliation and damage, too terrified to block the blows or run away?

She consulted her nature, what transcended memory, what couldn't be lost or forgotten, what was inborn and unchangeable.

It said, no way. If that man had abused her, emotionally or physically, she would have carved his brains out with forceps and sued him into his next few reincarnations.

So what did this mess mean?

"Are you okay?"

She shuddered miserably. "If feeling mad when I should be sad is okay. There must be more wrong with me than I realized."

After the surprise her words induced, contemplation settled on his face. "Anger *is* a normal reaction in your situation."

"What?" He knew why it was okay to feel so mad at a dead man?

"It's a common reaction for bereaved people to feel anger at their loved ones who die and leave them behind. It's worse when someone dies in an accident that that someone had a hand in or caused. The first reaction after shock and disbelief is rage, and it's all initially directed toward the victim. That also explains your earlier attack of bitterness. Your subconscious must have known that he was the one flying the plane. It might have recorded all the reports that flew around you at the crash site."

"You're saying I speak Spanish?"

He frowned. "Not to my knowledge. But maybe you approximated enough medical terminology to realize the extent of his injuries…."

"Ya lo sé hablar español."

She didn't know which of them was more flabbergasted.

The Spanish words had flowed from a corner in her mind to her tongue without conscious volition. And she certainly knew what they meant. *I know how to speak Spanish.*

"I…had no idea you spoke Spanish."

"Neither did I, obviously. But I get the feeling that the knowledge is partial…fresh."

"Fresh? How so?"

"It's just a feeling, since I remember no facts. It's like I've only started learning it recently."

He fixed her with a gaze that seeped into her skin, mingled into the rapids of her blood. Her temperature inched higher.

Was he thinking what she was thinking? That she'd started learning Spanish because of him? To understand his mother tongue, understand *him* better, to get closer to him?

At last he said, "Whatever the case may be, you evidently know enough Spanish to validate my theory."

He was assigning her reactions a perfectly human and natural source. Wonder what he'd say if she set him straight?

She bet he'd think her a monster. And she wouldn't blame him. She was beginning to think it herself.

Next second she was no longer thinking it. She knew it.

The memory that perforated her brain like a bullet was a visual. An image that corkscrewed into her marrow. The image of Mel, the husband she remembered with nothing but anger, whose death aroused only a mixture of resentment and liberation.

In a wheelchair.

Other facts dominoed like collapsing pillars, crushing everything beneath their impact. Not memories, just knowledge.

Mel had been paralyzed from the waist down. In a car accident. *During* their relationship. She didn't know if it had been before or after they'd gotten married. She didn't think it mattered.

She'd been right when she'd hypothesized why no one had rushed to her bedside. She was heartless.

What else could explain harboring such harshness toward someone who'd been so afflicted? The man she'd promised to love in sickness and in health? The one she'd basically felt "good riddance" toward when death *did* them part?

In the next moment, the air was sucked out of her lungs from a bigger blow.

"Cybele? *¿Te duele?*"

Her ears reverberated with the concern in Rodrigo's voice, her vision rippled over the anxiety warping his face.

No. She wasn't okay.

She was a monster. She was amnesic.

And she was pregnant.

Four

Excruciating minutes of dry retching later, Cybele lay surrounded by Rodrigo, alternating between episodes of inertness and bone-rattling shudders.

He soothed her with the steady pressure of his containment, wiping her eyelids and lips in fragrant coolness, his stroking persistent, hypnotic. His stability finally earthed her misery.

He tilted the face she felt had swollen to twice its original size to his. "You remembered something else?"

"A few things," she hiccuped, struggled to sit up. The temptation to lie in his arms was overwhelming. The urge only submerged her under another breaker of guilt and confusion.

He helped her sit up, then severed all contact, no doubt not wanting to continue it a second beyond necessary.

Needing to put more distance between them, she swung her numb legs to the floor, slipped into the downy slippers that were among the dozens of things he'd supplied for her comfort, things that felt tailored to her size and needs and desires.

She wobbled with her IV drip pole to the panoramic window overlooking the most amazing verdant hills she'd ever seen. Yet she saw nothing but Rodrigo's face, seared into her retinas, along with the vague but nausea-inducing images of Mel in his wheelchair, his rugged good looks pinched and pale, his eyes accusing.

She swung around, almost keeled over. She gasped, saw Rodrigo's body bunch like a panther about to uncoil in a flying leap. He was across the room, but he'd catch her if she collapsed.

She wouldn't. Her skin was crackling where he'd touched her. She couldn't get enough of his touch but couldn't let him touch her again. She held out a detaining hand, steadied herself.

He still rose but kept his distance, his eyes catching the afternoon sun, which poured in ropes of warm gold through the wall-to-wall glass. Their amalgamated color glowed as he brooded across the space at her, his eyebrows lowered, his gaze immobilizing.

She hugged her tender left shoulder, her wretchedness thickening, hardening, settling into concrete deadness. "The things I just remembered...I wouldn't call them real memories. At least, not when I compare them to the memories I've been accumulating since I regained consciousness. I remember those in Technicolor, frame by frame, each accompanied by sounds and scents and sensations. But the things I just recalled came in colorless, soundless and shapeless, like skeletons of data and knowledge. Like headings without articles. If that makes any sense."

He lowered his eyes to his feet, before raising them again, the surgeon in him assessing. "It makes plenty of sense. I've dealt with a lot of post-traumatic amnesia cases, studied endless records, and no one described returning memories with more economy and efficiency than you just did. But it's still early. Those skeletal memories will be fleshed out eventually…."

"I don't want them fleshed out. I want them to stop coming, I want what came back to disappear." She squeezed her shoulder, inducing more pain, to counteract the skewer turning in her gut. "They'll keep exploding in my mind until they blow it apart."

"What did you remember this time?"

Her shoulders sagged. "That Mel was a paraplegic."

He didn't nod or blink or breathe. He just held her gaze. It was the most profound and austere acknowledgment.

And she moaned the rest, "And I'm pregnant."

He blinked, slowly, the motion steeped in significance. He knew. And it wasn't a happy knowledge. Why?

One explanation was that she'd been leaving Mel, but he'd become paralyzed and she'd discovered her pregnancy and it had shattered their plans. Was that the origin of the antipathy she had felt radiating from him from time to time? Was he angry at her for leading him on then telling him that she couldn't leave her husband now that he was disabled and she was expecting his child?

She wouldn't know unless he told her. It didn't seem he was volunteering any information.

She exhaled. "Judging from my concave abdomen, I'm in the first trimester."

"Yes." Then as if against his better judgment, he added, "You're three weeks pregnant."

"Three *weeks*…? How on earth do you know that? Even if you had a pregnancy test done among others before my surgery, you can't pinpoint the stage of my pregnancy that accurate—" Her words dissipated under another gust of realization. "I'm pregnant through IVF. That's how you know how far along I am."

"Actually, you had artificial insemination. Twenty days ago."

"Don't tell me. You know the exact hour I had it, too."

"It was performed at 1:00 p.m."

She gaped at him, finding nothing to explain that too-specific knowledge. And the whole scenario of her pregnancy.

If it had been unplanned and she'd discovered it after she'd decided to leave Mel, that would still make her a cold-blooded two-timer. But it hadn't been unplanned. Pregnancies didn't come more planned than *that*. Evidently, she'd *wanted* to have a baby with Mel. So much that she'd made one through a procedure, when he could no longer make one with her the normal way. The intimate way.

So their marriage *had* been healthy. Until then. Which gave credence to Rodrigo's claim that they'd been planning a honeymoon. Maybe to celebrate her pregnancy.

So how come her first reaction to his death was bitter relief, and to her pregnancy such searing dismay?

What kind of twisted psyche did she have?

There was only one way to know. Rodrigo. He kept filling in the nothingness that had consumed most of what seemed to have been a maze of a life. But he was doing so reluctantly, cautiously, probably being of the school that thought providing another person's memories would make reclaiming hers more difficult, or would taint or distort them as they returned.

She didn't care. Nothing could be more tainted or distorted than her own interpretations. Whatever he told her would provide context, put it all in a better light. Make her someone she could live with. She had to pressure him into telling her what he knew....

Her streaking thoughts shrieked to a halt.

She couldn't *believe* she hadn't wondered. About *how* he knew what he knew. She'd let his care sweep her up, found his knowledge of her an anchoring comfort she hadn't thought to question.

She blurted out the questions under pressure. "Just how do you know all this? How do you know me? And Mel?"

The answer detonated in her mind.

It was that look in his eyes. Barely curbed fierceness leashed behind the steel control of the surgeon and the suave refinement of the man. She remembered *that* look. *Really* remembered it. Not after she'd kissed him. Long before that. In that life she didn't remember.

In that life, Rodrigo had despised her.

And it hadn't been because she'd led him on, then wouldn't leave Mel. It was worse. Far worse.

He'd been Mel's best friend.

The implications of this knowledge were horrifying.

However things had been before, or worse, *after* Mel had been disabled, if she'd exhibited her attraction to Rodrigo, then he had good reason to detest her. The best.

"You remembered."

She raised hesitant eyes at his rasp. "Sort of."

"Sort of? Now that's eloquent. More skeletal headlines?"

There was that barely contained fury again. She blinked back distress. "I remember that you were his closest friend, and that's how you know so much about us, down to the hour we had a procedure to conceive a baby. Sorry I can't do better." And she was damned if she'd ask him what the situation between *them* had been. She dreaded he'd verify her speculations. "I'm sure the rest will come back. In a flood or bit by bit. No need to hang around here waiting for either event. I want to be discharged."

He looked at her as if she'd sprouted two more sets of eyes. "Get back in bed, now, Cybele. Your lucidity is disintegrating with every moment on your feet, every word out of your mouth."

"Don't give me the patronizing medical tone, Dr. Valderrama. I'm a license-holding insider, if you remember."

"You mean if *you* remember, don't you?"

"I remember enough. I can recuperate outside this hospital."

"You can only under meticulous medical supervision."

"I can provide that for myself."

"You mean you don't 'remember' the age-proven adage that doctors make the worst patients?"

"It has nothing to do with remembering it, just not subscribing to it. I can take care of myself."

"No, you can't. But I will discharge you. Into my custody. I will take you to my estate to continue your recuperation."

His declaration took the remaining air from her lungs.

His custody. His estate. She almost swayed under the impact of the images that crowded her mind, of what both would be like, the temptation to jump into his arms and say *Yes, please*.

She had to say no. Get away from him. And fast. "Listen, I was in a terrible accident, but I got off pretty lightly. I would have died if you and your ultra-efficient medical machine hadn't intervened, but you did, and you fixed me. I'm fine."

"You're so far from fine, you could be in another galaxy."

It was just *wrong*. That he'd have a sense of humor, too. That it would surface now. And would pluck at her own humor strings.

She sighed at her untimely, inappropriate reaction. "Don't exaggerate. All I have wrong with me is a few missing memories."

"A few? Shall we make a list of what you do remember, those headlines with the vanished articles, and another of the volumes you've had erased and might never be able to retrieve, then revisit your definition of 'a few'?"

"Cute." And he was. In an unbearably virile and overruling way. "But at the rate I'm retrieving headlines, I'll soon have enough to fill said volumes."

"Even if you do, that isn't your only problem. You had a severe concussion with brain edema and subdural hematoma. I operated on you for ten hours. Half of those were with orthopedic and vascular surgeons as we put your arm back together. Ramón said it was the most intricate open reduction and internal fixation of his career, while Bianca and I had a hell of a time repairing your blood vessels and nerves. Afterward, you were comatose for three days and woke up with a total memory deficit. Right now your neurological status is suspect, your arm is useless, you have bruises and contusions from head to toe and you're in your first trimester. Your body will need double the time and effort to heal during this most physiologically demanding time. It amazes me you're talking, and that much, moving at all and not lying in bed disoriented and sobbing for more painkillers."

"Thanks for the rundown of my condition, but seems I'm more amazing than you think. I'm pretty lucid and I can talk as endlessly as *you* evidently can. And the pain is nowhere as bad as before."

"You're pumped full of painkillers."

"No, I'm not. I stopped the drip."

"What?" He strode toward her in steps loaded with rising tension. He inspected her drip, scowled down on her. "When?"

"The moment you walked out after your last inspection."

"That means you have no more painkillers in your system."

"I don't need any. The pain in my arm is tolerable now. I

think it was coming out of the anesthesia of unconsciousness that made it intolerable by comparison."

He shook his head. "I think we also need to examine your definition of 'pretty lucid.' You're not making sense to me. Why feel pain at all, when you can have it dealt with?"

"Some discomfort keeps me sharp, rebooting my system instead of lying in drug-induced comfort, which might mask some deterioration in progress. What about *that* doesn't make sense to you?"

He scowled. "I *was* wondering what kept you up and running."

"Now you know. *And* I vividly recall my medical training. I may be amnesic but I'm not reckless. I'll take every precaution, do things by the post-operative, post-trauma book...."

"I'm keeping you by my side until I'm satisfied that you're back to your old capable-of-taking-on-the-world self."

That silenced whatever argument she would have fired back.

She'd had the conviction that he didn't think much of her.

So he believed she was strong, but despised her because she'd come on stronger to him? Could she have done something so out-of-character? She abhorred infidelity, found no excuse for it. At least the woman who'd awakened from the coma did not.

Then he surprised her more. "I'm not talking about how you were when you were with Mel, but before that."

She didn't think to ask how he knew what she'd been like before Mel. She was busy dealing with the suspicion that he was right, that her relationship with Mel *had* derailed her.

More broad lines resurfaced. How she'd wanted to be nothing like her mother, who'd left a thriving career to serve the whims of Cybele's stepfather, how she'd thought she'd never marry, would have a child on her own when her career had become unshakable.

Though she didn't have a time line, she sensed that until months ago, she'd held the same convictions.

So how had she found herself married, at such a crucial time as her senior residency year, and pregnant, too? Had she loved Mel so much that she'd been so blinded? Had she had setbacks in her job in consequence, known things would keep going downhill and that was why she remembered him with all this resentment? Was that why she'd found an excuse to let her feelings for Rodrigo blossom?

Not that there could be an excuse for that.

But strangely, she wasn't sorry she was pregnant. In fact, that was what ameliorated this mess, the one thing she was looking forward to. That…and, to her mortification, being with Rodrigo.

Which was exactly why she couldn't accept his carte blanche proposal.

"Thank you for the kind offer, Rodrigo—"

He cut her off. "It's neither kind nor an offer. It's imperative and it's a decision."

Now *that* was a premium slice of unadulterated autocracy.

She sent up a fervent thank-you for the boost to her seconds-ago-nonexistent resistance. "Imperative or imperious? Decision or dictate?"

"Great language recall and usage. And take your pick."

"I think it's clear I already did. And whatever you choose to call your *offer*, I can't accept it."

"You mean you won't."

"Fine. If you insist on dissecting my refusal. I won't."

"It seems you *have* forgotten all about me, Cybele. If you remembered even the most basic things, you'd know that when I make a decision, saying no to me is not an option."

Cybele stared at him. Life was grossly, horribly unfair. How did one being end up endowed with all that?

And she'd thought he had it all before she'd seen him crook his lips in that I-click-my-fingers-and-all-sentient-beings-obey quasi smile.

Now there was one thought left in her mind. An urge. To get as far away from him as possible. Against all logic. And desire.

Her lips twisted, too. "I didn't get that memo. Or I 'forgot' I did. So *I* can say no to you. Consider it a one-off anomaly."

That tiger-like smirk deepened. "You can say what you want. I'm your surgeon and what *I* say goes."

The way he'd said *your surgeon*. Everything clamored inside her, wishing he was her anything-and-everything, for real.

She shook her head to disperse the idiotic yearnings. "I'll sign any waiver you need me to. I'm taking full responsibility."

"I'm the one taking full responsibility for you. If you do remember being a surgeon, you know that my being yours makes me second only to God in this situation. You have no say in God's will, do you?"

"You're taking the God complex too literally, aren't you?"

"My status in your case is an uncontestable fact. You're in my care and will remain there until I'm satisfied you no longer need it. The one choice I leave up to you is whether I follow you up in my home as my guest, or in my hospital as my patient."

Cybele looked away from his hypnotic gaze, his logic. But there was no escaping either. It *had* been desperation, wanting to get away from him. She *wasn't* in a condition to be without medical supervision. And who best to follow her up but her own surgeon? The surgeon who happened to be the best there was?

She knew he was. He was beyond the best. A genius. With billions and named-after-him revolutionary procedures and equipment to prove it.

But even had she been fit, she wouldn't have wanted to be

discharged. For where could she go but home? A home she recalled with nothing but dreariness?

And she didn't want to be with anyone else. Certainly not with her mother and family. She remembered them as if they were someone else's unwanted acquaintances. Disappointing and distant. Their own actions reinforced that impression. The sum total of their concern over her accident and Mel's death had been a couple of phone calls. When told she was fine, didn't need anything, it seemed they'd considered it an excuse to stop worrying—if they *had* been worried—dismiss her and return to their real interests. She didn't remember specifics from her life with them, but this felt like the final straw in a string of lifelong letdowns.

She turned her face to him. He was watching her as if he'd been manipulating her thoughts, steering her toward the decision he wanted her to make. She wouldn't put mental powers beyond him. What was one more covert power among the glaringly obvious ones?

She nodded her capitulation.

He tilted his awesome head at her. "You concede your need for my supervision?" He wanted a concession in words? Good luck with that. She nodded again. "And which will it be? Guest or patient?"

He wanted her to pick, now? She'd hoped to let things float for a couple of days, until she factored in the implications of being either, the best course of action….

Just great. A scrambled memory surely hadn't touched her self-deception ability. Seemed she had that in spades.

She knew what the best course of action was. She *should* say patient. Should stay in the hospital where the insanities he provoked in her would be curbed, where she wouldn't be able to act on them. She *would* say patient.

Then she opened her mouth. "As if you don't already know."

She barely held back a curse, almost took the sullen words back.

She didn't. She was mesmerized by his watchfulness, by seeing it evaporate in a flare of…something. Triumph?

She had no idea. It was exhausting enough trying to read her own thoughts and reactions. She wasn't up to fathoming his. She only hoped he'd say something superior and smirking. It might trip a fuse that would make her retreat from the abyss of stupidity and self-destructiveness, do what sense and survival were yelling for her to do. Remain here, remain a patient to him, nothing more.

"It'll be an honor to have you as my guest, Cybele." Distress brimmed as the intensity in his eyes drained, leaving them as gentle as his voice. It was almost spilling over when that arrogance she'd prayed for coated his face. "It's a good thing you didn't say 'patient,' though. I would have overruled you again."

She bristled. "Now look here—"

He smoothly cut across her offense. "I would have, because I built this center to be a teaching hospital, and if you stay, there is no way I can fairly stop the doctors and students from having constant access to you, to study your intriguing neurological condition."

Seemed not only did no one say no to him, no one ever won an argument with him, either. He'd given her the one reason that would send her rocketing out of this hospital like a cartoon character with a thick trail of white exhaust clouds in her wake.

No way would she be poked and prodded by med students and doctors-in-training. In the life that felt like a half-remembered documentary of someone else's, she'd been both, then the boss of a bunch of the latter. She knew how nothing—starting with patients' comfort, privacy, even basic human rights—stood in the way of acquiring their coveted-above-all experience.

She sighed. "You always get what you want, don't you?"

"No. Not always."

The tormented look that seized his face arrested her in midbreath. Was this about…her? Was *she* something he wanted and couldn't get?

No. She just knew what she felt for him had always been only on her side. On his, there'd been nothing inappropriate. He'd never given her reason to believe the feelings were mutual.

This…despondency was probably about failing to save Mel. That had to be the one thing he'd wanted most. And he hadn't gotten it.

She swallowed the ground glass that seemed to fill her throat. "I—I think I'll take a nap now."

He inhaled, nodded. "Yes, you do that."

He started to turn away, stopped, his eyes focusing far in the distance. He seemed to be thinking terrible things.

A heart-thudding moment later, without looking back again, he muttered, "Mel's funeral is this afternoon." She gasped. She'd somehow never thought of that part. He looked back at her then, face gripped with urgency, eyes storming with entreaty. "You should know."

She gave a difficult nod. "Thanks for telling me."

"Don't thank me. I'm not sure I should have."

"Why? You don't think I can handle it?"

"You seem to be handling everything so well, I'm wondering if this isn't the calm before the storm."

"You think I'll collapse into a jibbering mess somewhere down the road?"

"You've been through so much. I wouldn't be surprised."

"I can't predict the future. But I'm as stable as can be now. I—I want to go. I have to."

"You don't have to do anything, Cybele. Mel wouldn't have wanted you to go through the added trauma."

So Mel had cared for her? Wanted the best for her?

She inhaled, shook her head. "I'm coming. You're not going to play the not-neurologically-stable-enough card, are you?"

His eyes almost drilled a crater of conflicted emotions between her own. "You should be okay. If you do everything I say."

"And what is that?"

"Rest now. Attend the funeral in a wheelchair. And leave when I say. No arguments."

She hadn't the energy to do more than close her eyelids in consent. He hesitated, then walked back to her, took her elbow, guided her back to the bed. She sagged down on it.

He, too, dropped down, to his haunches. Heartbeats shook her frame as he took one numb foot after the other, slid off slippers that felt as if they were made of hot iron. He rose, touched her shoulder, didn't need to apply force. She collapsed like water in a fountain with its pressure lost. He scooped up her legs, swung them over the bed, swept the cotton cover over her, stood back and murmured, "Rest."

Without another look, he turned and crossed the room as if he'd been hit with a fast-forward button.

The moment the door clicked shut, shudders overtook her.

Rest? He really thought she could? After what he'd just done? Before she had to attend her dead husband's funeral?

She ached. For him, because of him, because she breathed, with guilt, with lack of guilt.

She could only hope that the funeral, the closure ritual, might open up the locked, pitch-black cells in her mind.

Maybe then she'd get answers. And absolution.

Five

She didn't rest.

Four hours of tossing in bed later, at the entry of a genial brunette bearing a black skirt suit and its accessories, Cybele staggered up feeling worse than when she'd woken from her coma.

She winced a smile of thanks at the woman and insisted she didn't need help dressing. Her fiberglass arm cast was quite light and she could move her shoulder and elbow joints well enough to get into the front-fastening jacket and blouse.

After the woman left, she stood staring at the clothes Rodrigo had provided for her. To attend the funeral of the husband she didn't remember. Didn't want to remember.

She didn't need help dressing. She needed help destressing.

No chance of that. Only thing to do was dress the part, walk in and out of this. Or rather, get wheeled in and out.

In minutes she was staring at her reflection in the full-wall mirror in the state-of-the-art, white and gray bathroom.

Black wool suit, white silk blouse, two-inch black leather shoes. All designer items. All made as if for her.

A knock on the door ripped her out of morbid musings over the origin of such accuracy in judging her size.

She wanted to dart to the door, snatch it open and yell, *Let's get it over with*.

She walked slowly instead, opened the door like an automaton. Rodrigo was there. With a wheelchair. She sat down without a word.

In silence, he wheeled her through his space-age center to a gigantic elevator that could accommodate ten gurneys and their attending personnel. This was obviously a place equipped and staffed to deal with mass casualty situations. She stared ahead as they reached the vast entrance, feeling every eye on her, the woman their collective boss was tending to personally.

Once outside the controlled climate of the center, she shivered as the late February coolness settled on her face and legs. He stopped before a gleaming black Mercedes 600, slipped the warmth of the cashmere coat she realized had been draped over his arm all along around her shoulders as he handed her into the back of the car.

In moments he'd slid in beside her on the cream leather couch, signaled the chauffeur and the sleek beast of a vehicle shot forward soundlessly, the racing-by vistas of the Spanish countryside the only proof that it was streaking through the nearly empty streets.

None of the beauty zooming by made it past the surface of her awareness. All deeper levels converged on him. On the turmoil in the rigidity of his profile, the coiled tension of his body.

And she couldn't bear it anymore. "I'm…so sorry."

He turned to her. "What are you talking about?"

The harshness that flickered in his eyes, around his lips made her hesitate. It didn't stop her. "I'm talking about Mel." His eyes seemed to lash out an emerald flare. She almost backed down, singed and silenced. She forged on. "About your loss." His jaw muscles convulsed then his face turned to rock, as if he'd sucked in all emotion, buried it where it would never resurface for anyone to see. "I don't remember him or our relationship, but you don't have that mercy. You've lost your best friend. He died on your table, as you struggled to save him…."

"As I *failed* to save him, you mean."

His hiss hit her like the swipe of a sword across the neck.

She nearly suffocated on his anguish. Only the need to drain it made her choke out, "You didn't fail. There was nothing you could have done." His eyes flared again, zapping her with the force of his frustration. "Don't bother contradicting me or looking for ways to shoulder a nonexistent blame. Everyone knew he was beyond help."

"And that's supposed to make me feel better? What if I don't want to feel better?"

"Unfounded guilt never did anyone any good. Certainly not the ones we feel guilty over."

"How logical you can be, when logic serves no purpose."

"I thought you advocated logic as what serves every purpose."

"Not in this instance. And what I feel certainly isn't hurting me any. I'm as fit as an ox."

"So you're dismissing emotional and psychological pain as irrelevant? I know that as surgeons we're mainly concerned with physical disorders, things we can fix with our scalpels, but—"

"But nothing. I'm whole and hearty. Mel is dead."

"Through no fault of yours!" She couldn't bear to see him

bludgeoning himself with pain and guilt that way. "That's the only point I'm making, the only one to *be* made here. I know it doesn't make his loss any less traumatic or profound. And I am deeply sorry for—everyone. You, Mel, his parents, our baby."

"But not yourself?"

"No."

The brittle syllable hung between them, loaded with too much for mere words to express, and the better for it, she thought.

Twenty minutes of silence later her heart hiccupped in her chest. They were entering a private airport.

With every yard deeper into the lush, grassy expanses, tentacles of panic slid around her throat, slithered into her mind until the car came to a halt a few dozen feet from the stairs of a gleaming silver Boeing 737.

She blindly reached out to steady herself with the one thing that was unshakeable in her world. Rodrigo.

His arm came around her at the same moment she sought his support, memories billowing inside her head like the sooty smoke of an oil-spill fire. "This is where we boarded the plane."

He stared down at her for a suspended moment before closing his eyes. "*Dios, lo siento,* Cybele—I'm so sorry. I didn't factor in what it would do to you, being here, where your ordeal began."

She snatched air into her constricted lungs, shook her head. "It's probably the right thing to do, bringing me here. Maybe it'll get the rest of my memories to explode back at once. I'd welcome that over the periodic detonations."

"I can't take credit for attempting shock therapy. We're here for Mel's funeral." She gaped at him. He elaborated. "It's not a traditional funeral. I had Mel's parents flown over from the States so they can take his body home."

She struggled to take it all in. Mel's body. Here. In that hearse over there. His parents. She didn't remember them. At all. They must be in the Boeing. Which had to be Rodrigo's. They'd come down, and she'd see them. And instead of a stricken widow they could comfort and draw solace from, they'd find a numb stranger unable to share their grief.

"Rodrigo…" The plea to take her back now, that she'd been wrong, couldn't handle this, congealed in her throat.

He'd turned his head away. A man and a woman in their early sixties had appeared at the jet's open door.

He reached for his door handle, turned to her. "Stay here."

Mortification filled her. She was such a wimp. He'd felt her reluctance to face her in-laws, was sparing her.

She couldn't let him. She owed them better than that. She'd owe any grieving parents anything she could do to lessen their loss. "No, I'm coming with you. And no wheelchair, please. I don't want them to think I'm worse than I am." He pursed his lips, then nodded, exited the car. In seconds he was on her side, handing her out. She crushed his formal suit's lapel. "What are their names?"

His eyes widened, as if shocked all over again at the total gaps in her memory. "Agnes and Steven Braddock."

The names rang distant bells. She hadn't known them long, or well. She was sure of that.

The pair descended as she and Rodrigo headed on an intercept course. Their faces became clearer with every step, setting off more memories. Of how Mel had looked in detail. And in color.

Her father-in-law had the same rangy physique and wealth of hair, only it was gray where Mel's had been shades of bronze. Mel had had the startlingly turquoise eyes of her mother-in-law.

She stopped when they were a few steps way. Rodrigo didn't.

He kept going, opened his arms, and the man and woman rushed right into them. The three of them merged into an embrace that squeezed her heart dry of its last cell of blood.

Everything hurt. Burned. She felt like strips were being torn out of her flesh. Acid filled her eyes, burned her cheeks.

The way he held them, the way they sought his comfort and consolation as if it was their very next breath, the way they all clung together... The way he looked, wide open and giving everything inside him for the couple to take their fill of, to draw strength from...

Just when she would have cried out *Enough—please*, the trio dissolved their merger of solace, turned, focused on her. Then Agnes closed the steps between them.

She tugged Cybele into a trembling hug, careful not to brush against her cast. "I can't tell you how worried we were for you. It's a prayer answered to see you so well." So well? She'd looked like a convincing postmortem rehearsal last time she'd consulted a mirror. But then, compared to Mel, she was looking great. "It's why we were so late coming here. Rodrigo couldn't deal with this, with anything, until you were out of danger."

"He shouldn't have. I can't imagine how you felt, having to put th-this off."

Agnes shook her head, the sadness in her eyes deepening. "Mel was already beyond our reach, and coming sooner would have served no purpose. You were the one who needed Rodrigo's full attention so he could pull you through."

"He did. And while everyone says he's phenomenal with all his patients, I'm sure he's gone above and beyond even by his standards. I'm as sure it's because I was Mel's wife. It's clear what a close friend of the whole family he is."

The woman looked at her as if she'd said Rodrigo was in reality a reptile. "But Rodrigo isn't just a friend of the family. He's our son. He's Mel's brother."

* * *

Cybele felt she'd stared at Agnes for ages, feeling her words reverberating in her mind in shock waves.

Rodrigo. Wasn't Mel's best friend. Was his brother. *How?*

"You didn't know?" Agnes stopped, tutted to herself. "What am I asking. Rodrigo told us of your memory loss. You've forgotten."

She hadn't. She was positive. This was a brand-new revelation.

Questions heaved and pitched in her mind, splashed against the confines of her skull until she felt they'd shatter it.

Before she could relieve the pressure, launch the first few dozen, Rodrigo and Steven closed in on them. Rodrigo stood back as Steven mirrored his wife's actions and sentiments.

"We've kept Cybele on her feet long enough," Rodrigo addressed the couple who claimed to be his parents. "Why don't you go back to the car with her, Agnes, while Steven and I arrange everything."

Agnes? Steven? He didn't call them mother and father?

She would have asked to be involved if she wasn't burning for the chance to be alone with Agnes, to get to the bottom of this.

As soon as they settled into the car, Cybele turned to Agnes. And all the questions jammed in her mind.

What would she ask? How? This woman was here to claim her son's body. What would she think, feel, if said son's widow showed no interest in talking about him and was instead panting to know all about the man who'd turned out to be his brother?

She sat there, feeling at a deeper loss than she had since she'd woken up in this new life. Rodrigo's chauffeur offered them refreshments. She parroted what Agnes settled on, mechanically sipped her mint tea every time Agnes did hers.

Suddenly Agnes started to talk, the sorrow that coated her face mingling with other things. Love. Pride.

"Rodrigo was six, living in an exclusively Hispanic community in Southern California, when his mother died in a factory accident and he was taken into the system. Two years later, when Mel was six, we decided that he needed a sibling, one we'd realized we'd never be able to give him."

So that was it. Rodrigo was adopted.

Agnes went on. "We took Mel with us while we searched, since our one criteria for the child we'd adopt was that he get along with Mel. But Mel antagonized every child we thought was suited to our situation, got them to turn nasty. Then Rodrigo was suggested to us. We were told he was everything Mel wasn't—responsible, resourceful, respectful, with a steady temperament and a brilliant mind. But we'd been told so many good things about other children and we'd given up hope that any child would pass the test of interaction with Mel. Then Rodrigo walked in.

"After he introduced himself in the little English he knew, enquired politely why we were looking for another child, he asked to be left alone with Mel. Unknown to both boys, we were taken to where children's meetings with prospective parents were monitored. Mel was at his nastiest, calling Rodrigo names, making fun of his accent, insulting his parentage and situation. We were mortified that he even knew those…words, and would use them so viciously. Steven thought he felt threatened by Rodrigo, as he had by any child we sought. I told him whatever the reason, I couldn't let Mel abuse the poor boy, that we'd been wrong and Mel didn't need a sibling but firmer treatment until he outgrew his sullenness and nastiness. He hushed me, asked me to watch. And I watched.

"Rodrigo had so far shown no reaction. By then, other boys had lashed out, verbally and physically, at Mel's bullying. But

Rodrigo sat there, watching him in what appeared to be deep contemplation. Then he stood up and calmly motioned him closer. Mel rained more abuse on him, but when he still didn't get the usual reaction, he seemed to be intrigued. I was certain Rodrigo would deck him and sneer *gotcha* or something. I bet Mel thought the same.

"We all held our breath as Rodrigo put a hand in his pocket. My mind streaked with worst-case scenarios. Steven surged up, too. But the director of the boys' home detained us. Then Rodrigo took out a butterfly. It was made of cardboard and elastic and metal springs and beautifully hand-painted. He wound it up and let it fly. And suddenly Mel was a child again, giggling and jumping after the butterfly as if it were real.

"We knew then that Rodrigo had won him over, that our search for a new son was over. I was shaking as we walked in to ask Rodrigo if he'd like to come live with us. He was stunned. He said no one wanted older children. We assured him that we did want him, but that he could try us out first. He insisted it was he who would prove himself to us. He turned and shook Mel's hand, told him he'd made other toys and promised to teach him how to make his own."

The images Agnes had weaved were overwhelming. The vision of Rodrigo as a child was painfully vivid. Self-possessed in the face of humiliation and adversity, stoic in a world where he had no one, determined as he proved himself worthy of respect.

"And did he teach him?" she asked.

Agnes sighed. "He tried. But Mel was short-fused, impatient, never staying with anything long enough for it to bear fruit. Rodrigo never stopped trying to involve him, get him to experience the pleasures of achievement. We loved him with all our hearts from the first day, but loved him more for how hard he tried."

"So your plan that a sibling would help Mel didn't work?"

"Oh, no, it did. Rodrigo did absorb a great deal of Mel's angst and instability. He became the older brother Mel emulated in everything. It was how Mel ended up in medicine."

"Then he must have grown out of his impatience. It takes a lot of perseverance to become a doctor."

"You really don't remember a thing about him, do you?" Now what did that mean? Before she pressed for an elaboration, Agnes sighed again. "Mel was brilliant, could do anything if only he set his mind to it. But only Rodrigo knew how to motivate him, to keep him in line. And when Rodrigo turned eighteen, he moved out."

"Why? Wasn't he happy with you?"

"He assured us that his need for independence had nothing to do with not loving us or not wanting to be with us. He confessed that he'd always felt the need to find his roots."

"And you feared he was only placating you?"

Agnes's soft features, which showed a once-great beauty lined by a life of emotional upheavals, spasmed with recalled anxiety. "We tried to help as he searched for his biological family, but his methods were far more effective, his instincts of where to look far sharper. He found his maternal relatives three years later and his grandparents were beside themselves with joy. Their whole extended family welcomed him with open arms."

Cybele couldn't think how anyone wouldn't. "Did he learn the identity of his father?"

"His grandparents didn't know. They had had a huge quarrel with his mother when she got pregnant and she wouldn't reveal the father's identity. She left home, saying she'd never return to their narrow-minded world. Once they had calmed down, they searched for her everywhere, kept hoping she'd come home. But they never heard from her again. They were devastated to learn their daughter was long dead, but ecstatic that Rodrigo had found them."

"And he changed his name from yours to theirs then?"

"He never took our name, just kept the name his mother had used. There were too many obstacles to our adopting him, and when he realized our struggles, he asked us to stop trying, said he knew we considered him our son and we didn't need to prove it to him. He was content to be our foster son to the world. He was eleven at the time. When he found his family, he still insisted *we* were his real family, since it was choice and love that bound us and not blood. He didn't legally take their names until he made sure we knew that it just suited his identity more to have his Catalan names."

"And you still thought he'd walk out of your life."

Agnes exhaled her agreement. "It was the worst day of my life when he told us that he was moving to Spain as soon as his medical training was over. I thought my worst fears of losing him had come true."

It struck Cybele as weird that Agnes didn't consider the day Mel had died the worst day of her life. But she was too intent on the story for the thought to take hold. "But you didn't lose him."

"I shouldn't have worried. Not with Rodrigo. I should have known he'd never abandon us, or even neglect us. He never stopped paying us the closest attention, was a constant presence in our lives—more so even than Mel, who lived under the same roof. Mel always had a problem expressing his emotions, and showed them with material, not moral, things. That's probably why he…he…" She stopped, looked away.

"He what?" Cybele tried not to sound rabid with curiosity. They were getting to some real explanation here. She knew it.

She almost shrieked with frustration when Agnes ignored her question, returned to her original topic. "Rodrigo continued to rise to greater successes but made sure we were there to share the joy of every step with him. Even when he moved here, he never let us or Mel feel that he was far away. He was constantly after us to move here, too, to start projects we've long dreamed of, offered us everything we'd need to establish them. But Mel said Spain was okay for vacations but he was a New Yorker and could never live anywhere else. Though it was a difficult decision, we decided to stay in the States with him. We thought he was the one who…needed our presence more. But we do spend chunks of every winter with Rodrigo, and he comes to the States as frequently as possible."

And she'd met him during those frequent trips. Over and over. She just knew it. But she was just as sure, no matter how spotty her memory was, that *this* story hadn't been volunteered by anyone before. She was certain she hadn't been told Rodrigo was Mel's foster brother. Not by Mel, not by Rodrigo.

Why had neither man owned up to this fact?

Agnes touched her good hand. "I'm so sorry, my dear. I shouldn't have gone on and on down memory lane."

And the weirdest thing was, Agnes's musings hadn't been about the son she'd lost, but the son she'd acquired thirty years ago. "I'm glad you did. I need to know anything that will help me remember."

"And did you? Remember anything?"

It wasn't a simple question to ascertain her neurological state. Agnes wanted to know something. Something to do with what she'd started to say about Mel then dropped, as if ashamed, as if too distressed to broach it.

"Sporadic things," Cybele said cautiously, wondering how to lead back to the thread of conversation she just knew would explain why she'd felt this way about Mel, and about Rodrigo.

Agnes turned away from her. "They're back."

Cybele jerked, followed Agnes's gaze, frustration backing

up in her throat. Then she saw Rodrigo prowling in those powerful, control-laden strides and the sight of him drowned out everything else.

Suddenly a collage of images became superimposed over his. Of her and Mel going out with Rodrigo and a different sexpot each time, women who'd fawned over him and whom he'd treated with scathing disinterest, playing true to his reputation as a ruthless playboy.

Something else dislodged in her mind, felt as if an image had moved from the obscurity of her peripheral vision into the clarity of her focus. How Mel had become exasperating around Rodrigo.

If these were true memories, they contradicted everything Agnes had said, everything she'd sensed about Rodrigo. They showed him as the one who was erratic and inconstant, who'd had a disruptive, not a stabilizing, effect on Mel. Could she have overlooked all that, and her revulsion toward promiscuous men, under the spell of his charisma? Or could that have been his attraction? The challenge of his unavailability? The ambition of being the one to tame the big bad wolf? Could she have been that perverse and stupid...?

"Are you ready, Agnes?"

Cybele lurched at the sound of Rodrigo's fathomless baritone.

Stomach churning with the sickening conjectures, she dazedly watched him hand Agnes out of the car. Then he bent to her.

"Stay here." She opened her mouth. A gentle hand beneath her jaw closed it for her. "No arguments, remember?"

"I want to do what you're all going to do," she mumbled.

"You've had enough. I shouldn't have let you come at all."

"I'm fine. Please."

That fierceness welled in his eyes again. Then he gave a curt nod, helped her out of the car.

She didn't only want to be there for these people to whom she felt such a powerful connection. She also hoped she'd get more answers from Agnes before she and Steven flew back home.

Cybele watched Rodrigo stride with Steven to the hearse, where another four men waited. One was Ramón Velázquez, her orthopedic surgeon and Rodrigo's best friend—for real—and partner.

Rodrigo and Ramón shared a solemn nod then opened the hearse's back door and slid the coffin out. Steven and the three other men joined in carrying it to the cargo bay of the Boeing.

Cybele stood transfixed beside Agnes, watching the grim procession, her eyes flitting between Rodrigo's face and Steven's. The same expression gripped both. It was the same one on Agnes's face. Something seemed...off about that expression.

Conjectures ping-ponged inside her head as everything seemed to fast-forward until the ritual was over, and Steven walked back with Rodrigo to join Agnes in hugging Cybele farewell. Then the Braddocks boarded the Boeing and Rodrigo led Cybele back to the Mercedes.

The car had just swung out of the airfield when she heard the roar of the jet's takeoff. She twisted around to watch it sail overhead before it hurtled away, its noise receding, its size diminishing.

And it came to her, why she knew that off expression. It was the exhausted resignation exhibited by families of patients who died after long, agonizing terminal illnesses. It didn't add up when Mel's death had been swift and shocking.

Something else became glaringly obvious. She turned to Rodrigo. He was looking outside his window.

She hated to intrude on the sanctity of his heartache. But she had to make sense of it all. "Rodrigo, I'm sorry, but—"

He rounded on her, his eyes simmering in the rays penetrating the mirrored window. "Don't say you're sorry again, Cybele."

"I'm sor—" She swallowed the apology he seemed unable to hear from her. "I was going to apologize for interrupting your thoughts. But I need to ask. *They* didn't ask. About my pregnancy."

He seemed taken aback. Then his face slammed shut. "Mel didn't tell them."

This was one answer she hadn't considered. Yet another twist. "Why? I can understand not telling them of our intention to have a baby this way, in case it didn't work. But after it did, why didn't he run to them with the news?"

His shrug was eloquent with his inability to guess Mel's motivations. With his intention to drop the subject.

She couldn't accommodate him. "Why didn't *you* tell them?"

"Because it's up to you whether or not to tell them."

"They're my baby's grandparents. Of course I want to tell them. If I'd realized they didn't know, I would have. It would have given them solace, knowing that a part of their son remains."

His jaw worked for a moment. Then he exhaled. "I'm glad you *didn't* bring it up. You're not in any shape to deal with the emotional fallout of a disclosure of this caliber. And instead of providing the solace you think it would have, at this stage, the news would have probably only aggravated their repressed grief."

But it *hadn't* been repressed grief she'd sensed from them.

Then again, what did she know? Her perceptions might be as scrambled as her memories. "You're probably right." *As usual,* she added inwardly. "I'll tell them when I'm back to normal and I'm certain the pregnancy is stable."

He lowered his eyes, his voice, and simply said, "Yes."

Feeling drained on all counts, she gazed up at him—the mystery that kept unraveling only to become more tangled. The anchor of this shifting, treacherous new existence of hers.

And she implored, "Can we go home now, please?"

Six

He took her home. His home.

They'd driven back from the airport to Barcelona city center. From there it had taken over an hour to reach his estate.

By the time they approached it at sunset, she felt saturated with the sheer beauty of the Catalan countryside.

Then they passed through the electronic, twenty-foot wrought iron gates, wound through the driveway, and with each yard deeper into his domain, she realized. There was no such thing as a limit to the capacity to appreciate beauty, to be stunned by it.

She turned her eyes to him. He'd been silent save for necessary words. She'd kept silent, too, struggling with the contradictions of what her heart told her and what her memories insisted on, with wanting to ask him to dispel her doubts.

But the more she remembered everything he'd said and done, everything everyone had said about him in the past days, the more only one conclusion made sense. Her memories had to be false.

He turned to her. After a long moment, he said, deep, quiet, "Welcome to Villa Candelaria, Cybele."

She swallowed past the emotions, yet her "Thank you" came out a tremulous gasp. She tried again. "When did you buy this place?"

"Actually, I built it. I named it after my mother."

The lump grew as images took shape and form. Of him as an orphan who'd never forgotten his mother until he one day was affluent enough to build such a place and name it after her, so her memory would continue somewhere outside of his mind and…

Okay, she'd start weeping any second now. Better steer this away from personal stuff. "This place looks…massive. Not just the building, but the land, too."

"It's thirty thousand square feet over twenty acres with a mile-long waterfront. Before you think I'm crazy to build all this for myself, I built it hoping it would become the home of many families, affording each privacy and land for whatever projects and pursuits they wished for. Not that it worked out that way."

The darkness that stained his face and voice seared her. He'd wished to surround himself with family. And he'd been thwarted at every turn, it seemed. Was he suffering from the loneliness and isolation she felt were such an integral part of her own psyche?

"I picked this land completely by chance. I was driving once, aimlessly, when I saw that crest of a hill overlooking this sea channel." She looked where he was pointing. "The vision slammed into my mind fully formed. A villa built into those rock formations as if it was a part of them."

She reversed the process, imagining those elements without

the magnificent villa they now hugged as if it *were* an intrinsic part of their structure. "I always thought of the Mediterranean as all sandy beaches."

"Not this area of the northern Iberian coastline. Rugged rock is indigenous here."

The car drew to a smooth halt in front of thirty-foot wide stone steps among landscaped, terraced plateaus that surrounded the villa from all sides.

In seconds Rodrigo was handing her out and insisting she sit in the wheelchair she hadn't used much today. She acquiesced, wondered as he wheeled her up the gentle slope beside the steps if it had always been there, for older family members' convenience, or if it had been installed to accommodate Mel's condition.

Turning away from futile musings, she surrendered to the splendor all around her as they reached a gigantic patio that surrounded the villa. On one side it overlooked the magnificent property that was part vineyards and orchards and part landscaped gardens, with the valley and mountains in the distance, and on the other side, the breathtaking sea and shoreline.

The patio led to the highest area overlooking the sea, a massive terrace garden that was illuminated by golden lights planted everywhere like luminescent flowers.

He took her inside and she got rapid impressions of the interior as he swept her to the quarters he'd designated for her.

She felt everything had been chosen with an eye for uniqueness and comfort, simplicity and grandeur, blending sweeping lines and spaces with bold wall colors, honey-colored ceilings and furniture that complemented both. French doors and colonial pillars merged seamlessly with the natural beauty of hardwood floors accentuated by marble and granite. She knew she could spend weeks poring over every detail, but in its whole, she felt this was a place this formidable man had wanted his family to love, to feel at home in from the moment they set foot in it. She knew *she* did. And she hadn't technically set foot in it yet.

Then she did. He opened a door, wheeled her in then helped her out of the chair. She stood as he wheeled the chair to one side, walked out to haul in two huge suitcases that had evidently been transported right behind them.

He placed one on the floor and the other on a luggage stand at the far side of the room, which opened into a full-fledged dressing room.

She stood mesmerized as he walked back to her.

He was overwhelming. A few levels beyond that.

He stopped before her, took her hand. She felt as though it burst in flames. "I promise you a detailed tour of the place. Later. In stages. Now you have to rest. Doctor's orders."

With that he gave her hand a gentle press, turned and left.

The moment the door clicked closed behind him, she staggered to lean on it, exhaled a choppy breath.

Doctor's orders. *Her* doctor…

She bit her lip. Hours ago, she'd consigned her husband's body to his parents. And all she could think of was Rodrigo. There wasn't even a twinge of guilt toward Mel. There *was* sadness, but it was the sadness she knew she'd feel for any human being's disability and death. For his loved ones' mourning. Nothing more.

What was wrong with her? What had been wrong with her and Mel? Or was there more wrong with her mind than she believed?

Her lungs deflated on a dejected exhalation.

All she could do now was never let any of those who'd loved and lost Mel know how unaffected by his loss she was. What did it matter what she felt in the secrecy of her heart and mind if she never let the knowledge out to hurt others? She couldn't change the way she felt, should stop feeling bad about it. It served no purpose, did no one any good.

With that rationalization reached, she felt as if a ten-pound rock had been lifted off her heart. Air flowed into her lungs all of a sudden, just as the lovely surroundings registered in her appreciation centers.

The room—if a thirty-something- by forty-something-foot space with a twelve-foot ceiling could be called that—was a manifestation of the ultimate in personal space.

With walls painted sea-blue and green, furniture of dark mahogany and ivory ceilings and accents, it was soothingly lit by golden lamps of the side and standing variety. French doors were draped in gauzy powder-blue curtains that undulated in the twilight sea breeze, wafting scents of salt and freshness with each billow. She sighed away her draining tension and pushed from the wood-paneled door.

She crossed the gleaming hardwood floor to the suitcases. They were more evidence of Rodrigo's all-inclusive care. She was certain she'd never owned anything so exquisite. She wondered what he'd filled them with. If the outfit she had on was any indication, no doubt an array of haute couture and designer items, molding to her exact shape and appealing to her specific tastes.

She tried to move the one on the floor, just to set it on its wheels. Frantic pounding boomed in her head.

Man—what *had* he gotten her to wear? Steel armor in every shade? And he'd made the cases look weightless when he'd hauled them both in, simultaneously. She tugged again.

"¡Parada!"

She swung around at the booming order, the pounding in her head crashing down her spine to settle behind her ribs.

A robust, unmistakably Spanish woman in her late thirties was plowing her way across the room, alarm and displeasure furrowing the openness of her olive-skinned beauty.

"Rodrigo warned me that you'd give me a hard time."

Cybele blinked at the woman as she slapped her hand away from the suitcase's handle and hauled it onto the king-sized, draped-in-ivory-silk bed. She, too, made it look so light. Those Spaniards—uh, Catalans—must have something potent in their water.

The woman rounded on her, vitality and ire radiating from every line. Even her shoulder-length, glossy dark brown hair seemed pissed off. "He told me that you'd be a troublesome charge, and from the way you were trying to bust your surgery scar open, he was right. As he always is."

So it wasn't only she who thought he was always practically infallible. Her lips tugged as she tried to placate the force of nature before her. "I don't have a surgery scar to bust, thanks to Rodrigo's revolutionary minimally invasive approach."

"You have things in there—" the woman stabbed a finger in the air pointing at Cybele's head "—you can bust, no? What you busted before, necessitating such an approach."

From the throb of pain that was only now abating, she had to concede that. She'd probably raised her intracranial pressure tenfold trying to drag that behemoth of a bag. As she shrugged, she remembered Rodrigo telling her something.

She'd been too busy watching his lips wrap around each syllable to translate the words into an actual meaning. She now replayed them, made sense of them.

Rodrigo had said Consuelo, his cousin who lived here with her husband and three children and managed the place for him, would be with her shortly to see to her every need and to the correct and timely discharge of his instructions. She'd only nodded then, lost in his eyes. She now realized what he'd meant.

He didn't trust her to follow his instructions, was assigning a deputy to enforce their execution. And he certainly knew how to pick his wardens.

She stuck out her hand with a smile tugging at her lips. "You must be Consuelo. Rodrigo told me to expect you."

Consuelo took her hand, only to drag her forward and kiss her full on both cheeks.

Cybele didn't know what stunned her more, the affectionate salute, or Consuelo resuming her disapproval afterward.

Consuelo folded her arms over an ample bosom artfully contained and displayed by her floral dress with the lime background. "Seems Rodrigo didn't *really* tell you what to expect. So let *me* make it clear. I received you battered and bruised. I'm handing you back in tip-top shape. *I* won't put up with you not following Rodrigo's orders. I'm not soft and lenient like him."

"Soft and lenient?" Cybele squeaked her incredulity. Then she coughed it out on a laugh. "I wasn't aware there were two Rodrigos. I met the intractable and inexorable one."

Consuelo tutted. "If you think Rodrigo intractable and inexorable, wait till you've been around me twenty-four hours."

"Oh, the first twenty-four seconds were a sufficient demo."

Consuelo gave her an assessing look, shrewdness simmering in her dark chocolate eyes. "I know your type. A woman who wants to do everything for herself, says she can handle it when she can't, keeps going when she shouldn't, caring nothing about what it costs her, and it's all because she dreads being an imposition, because she hates accepting help even when she dearly needs it."

"Whoa. Spoken like an expert."

"*¡Maldita sea, es cierto!*—that's right. It takes one mule-headed, aggravatingly independent woman to know another."

Another laugh overpowered Cybele. "Busted."

"*Sí,* you are. And I'm reporting your reckless behavior to Rodrigo. He'll probably have you chained to my wrist by your good arm until he gives you a clean bill of health."

"Not that I wouldn't be honored to have you as my...uh, keeper, but can I bribe you into keeping silent?"

"You can. And you know how."

"I don't try to lift rock-filled suitcases again?"

"And do everything I say. *When* I say it."

"Uh...on second thought, I'll take my chances with Rodrigo."

"Ha. Try another one. Now hop to it. Rodrigo told me what kind of day—what kind of *week* you've had. You're doing absolutely nothing but sleeping and resting for the next one. And eating. You look like you're about to vanish."

Cybele laughed as she whimsically peered down at her much lesser endowments. She could see how they were next to insubstantial by the super-lush Consuelo's standards.

This woman would be good for her. As she was sure Rodrigo had known she would be. Every word out of her mouth tickled funny bones Cybele hadn't known existed.

Consuelo hooked her arm through Cybele's good one, walked her to bed then headed alone to the en suite bathroom. She talked all the time while she ran a bubble bath, emptied the suitcases, sorted everything in the dressing room, and laid out what Cybele would wear to bed. Cybele loved listening to her husky, vibrant voice delivering perfect English dipped in the molasses of her all-out Catalan accent. By the time she led Cybele to the all-marble-and-gold-fixtures, salonlike bathroom, she'd told her her life story. At least, everything that had happened since she and her husband had become Rodrigo's house- and groundskeepers.

Cybele insisted she could take it from there. Consuelo insisted on leaving the door open. Cybele insisted she'd call out to prove she was still awake. Consuelo threatened to barge in after a minute's silence. Cybele countered she could sing to prove her wakefulness then everyone within hearing distance would suffer the consequences of Consuelo's overprotection.

Guffawing and belting out a string of amused Catalan, Consuelo finally exited the bathroom.

Grinning, Cybele undressed. The grin dissolved as she stared at herself in the mirror above the double sinks' marble platform.

She had a feeling there'd once been more of her. Had she lost weight? A lot of it? Recently? Because she'd been unhappy? If she had been, why had she planned a pregnancy and a second honeymoon with Mel? What did Rodrigo think of the way she looked? Not now, since she looked like crap, but before? Was she his type? Did he have a type? Did he have a woman now? More than one…?

Oh, God…she couldn't finish a thought without it settling back on him, could she?

She clamped down on the spasm that twisted through her at the idea, the images of him with a woman…any other woman.

How insane was it to be jealous, when up to eight days ago she'd been married to his brother?

She exhaled a shuddering breath and stepped into the warm, jasmine-and-lilac-scented water. She moaned as she submerged her whole body, felt as if every deep-seated ache surged to her surface, bled through her pores to mingle with the bubbles and fluid silk that enveloped her.

She raised her eyes, realized the widescreen window was

right across from her, showcasing a masterpiece of heavenly proportions. Magnificent cloud formations in every gradation of silver morphing across a darkening royal blue sky and an incandescent half moon.

Rodrigo's face superimposed itself on the splendor, his voice over the lapping of water around her, the swishing of blood in her ears. She shut her eyes, tried to sever the spell.

"Enough."

Consuelo's yelled *"¿Qué?"* jerked Cybele's eyes open.

Mortification threatened to boil her bathwater.

God—she'd cried that out loud.

She called out the first thing that came to her, to explain away her outburst. "Uh…I said I'm coming out. I've had enough."

And she had. In so many ways. But there was one more thing that she prayed she would soon have enough of. Rodrigo.

Any bets she never would?

It was good to face her weakness. Without self-deception, she'd be careful to plan her actions and control her responses, accept and expect no more than the medical supervision she was here for during her stay. Until it came to an end.

As it inevitably would.

Rodrigo stood outside Cybele's quarters, all his senses converged on every sound, every movement transmitted from within.

He'd tried to walk away. He couldn't. He'd leaned on her door, feeling her through it, tried to contain the urge to walk back in, remain close, see and hear and feel for himself that she was alive and aware.

The days during which she'd lain inert had gouged a fault line in his psyche. The past days since she'd come back, he hadn't been able to contemplate putting more than a few minutes' distance between them. It had been all he could do not to camp out in her room as he had during her coma. He had constantly curbed himself so he wouldn't suffocate her with worry, counted down every second of the three hours he'd imposed on himself between visits.

After he'd controlled the urge, he'd summoned Consuelo, had dragged himself away. Then he'd heard Consuelo's shout.

He hadn't barged into the room only because he'd frozen with horror for the seconds it took him to realize Consuelo had exclaimed *Stop*, and Consuelo's gregarious tones and Cybele's gentler, melodic ones had carried through the door, explaining the whole situation.

Now he heard Cybele's raised voice as she chattered with Consuelo from the bathroom. In a few minutes, Consuelo would make sure Cybele was tucked in bed and would walk out. He had to be gone before that. Just not yet.

He knew he was being obsessive, ridiculous, but he couldn't help it. The scare was too fresh, the trauma too deep.

He hadn't been there for Mel, and he'd died.

He had to be there for Cybele.

But to be there for her, he had to get ahold of himself. And to do that, he had to put today behind him.

It had felt like spiraling down through hell. Taking her to that airfield, realizing too late what he'd done, seeing his foster parents after months of barely speaking to them, only to give them the proof of his biggest failure. Mel's body.

The one thing mitigating this disaster was Cybele's memory loss. It *was* merciful. For her. For him, too. He didn't know if he could have handled her grief, too, had she remembered Mel.

But—was it better to have reprieve now, than to have it all come back with a vengeance later? Wouldn't it have been better if her grief coincided with his? Would he be able to bear it, to be of any help if she fell apart when he'd begun healing?

But then he had to factor in the changes in her.

The woman who'd woken up from the coma was not the Cybele Wilkinson he'd known the past year. Or the one Mel had said had become so volatile, she'd accused him of wanting her around only as the convenient help rolled into one with a medical supervisor—and who'd demanded a baby as proof that he valued her as his wife.

Rodrigo had at first found that impossible to believe. She'd never struck him as insecure or clingy. Just the opposite. But then her actions had proved Mel right.

So which persona was really her? The stable, guileless woman she'd been the past five days? The irritable introvert she'd been before Mel's accident? Or the neurotic wreck who'd made untenable emotional demands of him when he'd been wrecked himself?

And if this new persona was a by-product of the accident, of her injuries, once she healed, once she regained all her memories, would she revert? Would the woman who was bantering so naturally with Consuelo, who'd consoled him and wrestled verbally with him and made him forget everything but her, disappear?

He forced himself away from the door. Consuelo was asking what Cybele would like for breakfast. In a moment she'd walk out.

He strode away, speculations swarming inside his head.

He was staring at the haggard stranger in mourning clothes in his bathroom mirror when he realized something.

It made no difference. Whatever the answers were, no matter what she was, or what would happen from now on, it didn't matter.

She was in his life now. To stay.

Seven

"You don't have post-traumatic amnesia."

Cybele's eyes rounded at Rodrigo's proclamation.

Her incredulity at his statement was only rivaled by the one she still couldn't get over; that he'd transferred a miniature hospital to his estate so he could test and chart her progress daily.

Apart from wards and ORs, he had about everything else on site. A whole imaging facility with X-ray, MRI, CT machines and even a PET scan machine, which seemed like overkill just to follow up her arm's and head's healing progress. A comprehensive lab for every known test to check up on her overall condition and that of her pregnancy. Then there were the dozen neurological tests he subjected her to daily, plus the physiotherapy sessions for her fingers.

They'd just ended such a session and were heading out to the barbecue house at the seafront terrace garden to have lunch, after which he'd said they'd explore more of the estate.

He was walking beside her, his brows drawn together, his eyes plastered to the latest batch of results from another dozen tests. So what did he mean, she didn't have…?

Terrible suspicion mushroomed, clouding the perfection of the day.

Could he think she'd capitalized on a transient memory loss and had been stringing him along for the past four weeks? Or worse, that she'd never had memory loss, that she was cunning enough, with a convoluted enough agenda, to have faked it from the start?

And she blurted it out, "You think I'm pretending?"

"What?" He raised his eyes sluggishly, stared ahead into nothingness as if the meaning of her words was oozing through his mind, searching for comprehension. Then it hit him. Hard. His head jerked toward her, his frown spectacular. *"No."*

She waited for him to elaborate. He didn't, buried his head back into the tests.

So she prodded. "So what do you mean I don't have PTA? I woke up post-trauma with amnesia. Granted, it's not a classic case, but what else could it be?"

Instead of answering, he held the door of the terrace pergola open for her. She stepped out into the late March midday, barely stopped herself from moaning as the sweet saltiness of the sea breeze splashed her face, weaved insistent fingers through her hair.

He looked down at her as they walked, as if he hadn't heard her question. She shivered, not from the delicious coolness of the wind, but from the caress of his gaze, which followed the wind's every movement over her face and through her hair.

At least, that was how it felt to her. It was probably all in her mind, and he was lost in thought and not seeing her at all.

He suddenly turned his eyes again to the tests, validating her interpretation. "Let's review your condition, shall we? You started out having total retrograde amnesia, with all the memories formed before the accident lost. Then you started retrieving 'islands of memory,' when you recalled those 'skeletal' events. But you didn't suffer from any degree of anterograde amnesia, since you had no problems creating new memories after the injury. Taking all that into account, and that it has been over four weeks and the 'islands' have not coalesced into a uniform landmass…"

"As uniform as could be, you mean," she interrupted. "Even so-called healthy people don't remember everything in their lives—most things not in reliable detail and some things not at all."

"Granted. But PTA that lasts that long indicates severe brain injury, and it's clear from your clinical condition and all of your tests that you are not suffering from any cognitive, sensory, motor or coordination deficits. An isolated PTA of this magnitude is unheard of. That is why I'm leaning toward diagnosing you with a hybrid case of amnesia. The trauma might have triggered it, but the major part of your memory deficit is psychogenic, not organic."

She chewed her lip thoughtfully. "So we're back to what I said minutes after I regained consciousness. I *wanted* to forget."

"Yes. You diagnosed yourself fresh out of a coma."

"It wasn't really a diagnosis. I was trying to figure out why I had no other symptoms. When I didn't find an explanation, I thought either my medical knowledge had taken a hit, or that neurology was never my strong point in my parallel existence. I thought you would know that cases like mine exist. But they don't. Turns out I don't really have amnesia, I'm just hysterical."

His gaze whipped to hers, fierce, indignant. "Psychogenic

amnesia is no less real than organic. It's a self-preservation mechanism. I also wouldn't label the psychogenic ingredient of your memory loss as hysterical, but rather functional or dissociative. In fact, I don't support the hysterical nomenclature and what it's come to be associated with—willful and weak-willed frenzy."

Hot sweetness unfurled inside her. He was defending her to herself. Pleasure surged to her lips, making them tingle. "So you think I have a repressed-memory type functional amnesia."

He nodded, ultraserious. "Yes. Here, take a look at this. This is your last MRI." She looked. "It's called functional imaging. After structural imaging revealed no physical changes in your brain, I looked at the function. You see this?" She did. "This abnormal brain activity in the limbic system led to your inability to recall stressful and traumatic events. The memories are stored in your long-term memory, but access to them has been impaired through a mixture of trauma and psychological defense mechanisms. The abnormal activity explains your partial memory recovery. But now that I'm certain there's nothing to worry about organically, I'm relaxed about when total recovery occurs."

"*If* it ever does." If he was right, and she couldn't think how he wasn't, she might be better off if it never did.

Psychogenic amnesia sufferers included soldiers and childhood abuse, rape, domestic violence, natural disaster and terrorist attack victims. Sufferers of severe enough psychological stress, internal conflict or intolerable life situations. And if her mind had latched on to the injury as a trigger to purge her memories of Mel and her life with him, she'd probably suffered all three.

But that still didn't explain her pregnancy or the honeymoon they were heading to when they'd had the accident.

Rodrigo stemmed the tide of confusion that always overcame her when she came up against those points.

"Anyway," he said. "While explanations have been proposed to explain psychogenic amnesia, none of them have been verified as the mechanism that fits all types. I prefer to set aside the Freudian, personal semantic belief systems and betrayal trauma theories to explain the condition. I lean toward the theory that explains the biochemical imbalance that triggers it."

"That's why you're a neurosurgeon and not a neurologist or psychiatrist. Where others are content to deal with insults to the psyche, you dig down to the building blocks of the nervous system, cell by cell, neurotransmitter by neurotransmitter."

"I admit, I like to track any sign or symptom, physical or psychological, back to its causative mechanism, to find the 'exactly how' after others explain the 'why.'"

"And that's why you're a researcher and inventor."

He focused on her eyes for a second before he turned his own back to the tests, his skin's golden-bronze color deepening.

He was embarrassed!

She'd noticed on many occasions that, although he was certain of his abilities, he wasn't full of himself and didn't expect or abide adulation, despite having every reason to feel superior and to demand and expect being treated as such.

But this—to actually blush at her admiration! Oh, Lord, but he was delicious, scrumptious. Edible. And adorable.

And he ignored her praise pointedly. "So—I favor the theory that postulates that normal autobiographical memory processing is blocked by altered release of stress hormones in the brain during chronic stress conditions. With the regions of expanded limbic system in the right hemisphere more vulnerable to stress and trauma, affecting the body's opioids, hormones and neurotransmitters, increased levels of glucocorticoid and mineralocorticoid receptor density affect the anterior temporal, orbitofrontal cortex, hippocampal and amygdalar regions."

She couldn't help it. Her lips spread so wide they hurt. "I bet you're having a ball talking to a doctor/patient. Imagine all the translation into layman's terms you'd have to do if you wanted to say *that* to someone who didn't get the lingo."

He blinked, surprise tingeing his incredible eyes. Then that incendiary smile of his flowed over his face, crooked his divine-work-of-art lips. "It has been a very freeing experience, spoiling even, not to keep looking for ways to explain what I'm doing or what's happening and fearing I won't be clear enough or that you'll misinterpret it no matter what I say and develop false expectations, positive or negative." He shook his head in self-deprecation, switching back to solemn in a blink. "But that was far too involved, anyway. My point is, you might have appeared or thought you were coping with your situation before the accident, but according to your current condition, you weren't."

She pursed her lips in an effort to stop herself from grinning uncontrollably and giving in to the urge to lunge at him, tickle him out of his seriousness. "So you're saying I was headed for psychogenic amnesia, anyway?"

"No, I'm saying the unimaginable stress of experiencing a plane crash, plus the temporary brain insult you suffered, disrupted the balance that would have kept your memory intact in the face of whatever psychological pressure you were suffering."

She raised an eyebrow, mock-indignant. "You're trying very hard to find neurologically feasible explanations backed by complex theories and medical expressions to dress up the fact that you've diagnosed me as a basket case, aren't you?"

"No! I certainly haven't. You're in no way…" He stopped abruptly when she couldn't hold back anymore, let the smile split her face. Incredulity spread over his face. "You're playing me!"

She burst out laughing. "Yep. For quite some time now. But you were so involved in your explanations, so careful not to give me any reason to feel silly or undeserving of concern or follow-up since my condition is 'only in my mind,' you didn't notice."

One formidable eyebrow rose, a calculating gleam entering his eyes, an unbearably sexy curl twisting his lips. "Hmm, seems I have underestimated the stage of your progress."

"Been telling you so for—"

"Quite some time now. Yes, I get it. But now that I'm certain your brain is in fine working order, nuts-and-bolts-wise, being the guy who cares about nothing but the hardware, I think I can safely stop treating you like you're made of fresh paint."

A laugh cracked out of her at his metaphor. He kept surprising her. She'd be thinking he was this ultra-cerebral, all-work genius of a man, then out of the blue, he'd let this side of him show. The most witty and wickedly fun person she'd ever known. And she did know that for a fact. She remembered all of her life before Mel now.

She pretended to wipe imaginary sweat off her brow. "Phew, I thought I'd never get you to stop."

"Don't be so happy. Until minutes ago, I would have let you trampoline-jump all over me. Now I think you don't warrant the walking-on-eggshells preferential treatment anymore. You deserve some punishment for making fun of my efforts to appear all-knowing."

"Making fun of them, or debunking them?"

"Payback is getting steeper by the word."

She made a cartoonish face. "What can you do to a poor patient who has expanded limbic system issues and increased levels of glucocorticoid and mineralocorticoid receptor density messing with her anterior temporal, orbitofrontal cortex, hippocampal and amygdalar regions?"

"That's it. I'm exacting retribution."

"What will you do? Make me go to my room?"

"I'll make you eat what I cook. And that's for starters. I'll devise something heinous while phase one is underway."

"You mean *more* heinous than your cooking?"

He rumbled something from his gut, devilry igniting in his eyes. She giggled and rushed ahead, felt like she was flying there, borne on the giddy pleasure of his pursuing chuckles.

When she reached the steps, his voice boomed behind her, concern gripping its rich power. "Slow down."

She did, waited for him to catch up with her in those strides that ate up ten of her running steps in five.

She grinned up into his no-longer-carefree, admonishing eyes. "I thought I wasn't getting the fresh-paint treatment any longer."

"You've hereby moved to getting the uninsured, last-known-piece-of-Ming-dynasty-China treatment."

He slipped a steadying hand around her waist as they scaled the steps. She felt she'd be secure if the whole country fell into the sea. Or he'd clasp her to his body and take off into the sky.

She leashed her desire to press into him. "Aha! I should have known you'd default on your declaration of my independence."

He grinned down at her as they reached the barbecue house. "Tales of your independence *have* been wildly exaggerated."

She made a face, ducked under the shade of the canvas canopy.

He gave her a smug look as he seated her, then went to the kitchen area and began preparing her "punishment."

She watched his every graceful move as putting out cooking

utensils and food items and chopping and slicing were turned into a precision performance like his surgeries. When he ducked inside to get more articles, she exhaled at the interruption of her viewing pleasure, swept her gaze to the sparkling azure-emerald waters of the magnificent, channellike part of the sea, the mile-long breathtaking sandy beach ensconced in a rocky hug.

The living, breathing tranquility imbued her. Most of the time she couldn't remember how she'd come to be here, or that she'd ever been anywhere else, that a world existed outside.

This place wasn't just a place. It was an…experience. A sense of completion, of arrival. A realm in time and space she'd never seen approximated, let alone replicated. An amalgam of nature's pristine grandeur and man's quest for the utmost in beauty and comfort. But all this would have been nothing without him.

It was being with him that made it embody heaven.

During the past weeks they'd made real fires, collected ripe fruits and vegetables, eaten their meals in the apartment-sized kitchen or in the cool barbecue house and held their after-dinner gatherings and entertainment in its lounge or in the huge pergola terrace.

She'd watched him play tennis on the floodlit court with the tireless Gustavo, swim endless laps in the half-Olympic-sized pool, drooled over his every move, longed to tear off her cast and shed her aches and throw herself into that pool after him….

"Ready for your punishment?"

She twinkled up at him. "Is it too heinous?"

He looked down at the salad bowls in his hands. "Atrocious."

"Gimme." She took her bowl, set it in front of her. And gaped. Then she crooked a challenging smile up at him. "It's colorful, I'll give you that. And…odorous." She tried not to wince as she picked up her fork. "*And* I didn't know these food items could go together."

He sat down across from her. "I didn't hear any objections as I tossed them into each other's company."

She chuckled. "I don't even know what said food items are."

His glance said her delaying tactics weren't working. "Eat."

She took a mouthful, trying not to inhale the stench, trying not to have what produced it hit her taste buds, to slide directly into her throat. Then it did hit, everywhere. And...wow.

She raised incredulous eyes to him. "You better get this patented. It's a-maaazing!"

He raised both eyebrows in disbelief. "You're just trying to prove nothing can gross you out, that I didn't and wouldn't succeed in punishing you, 'cause you can take anything."

"What am I, twelve?" She wolfed down another huge forkful.

He crooked his head to one side, considering. "So you like it."

"I love it," she exclaimed, mumbling around the food she'd stuffed into her mouth. "I *can* do without the smell, but it actually lessens as you eat, or your senses forgive it for being coupled with the delicious taste. At first I thought it was rotten fish."

"It *is* rotten fish."

She almost choked. "Now you're pulling my leg."

"Nope." The wattage of the wickedness in his eyes reached electrocuting levels. "But if you like it, does the label matter?"

She thought about that for a second, then said "Nah" and stuffed another forkful into her mouth.

He laughed as he began to eat his own serving. "It's actually only *semi*-rotten. It's called *feseekh*—sun dried then salted gray mullet. It's considered an acquired taste—which you must be the quickest to ever acquire—and a delicacy around here. It came to Catalonia with the Berbers, and they brought it all the way from Egypt. But I bet I'm the first one to mix it with a dozen unnamed leafy greens and the wild berries Gustavo grows and collects and gives to me to consume, assuring me they're the secret to my never needing any of our esteemed colleagues' services."

"So you can give me rotten and unidentified food to consume, but you balk at my walking faster than a turtle."

"The rotten ingredient has proved through centuries of folk experience to have potent antibacterial and digestive-regulating properties. It and the rest of the unidentified food have been repeatedly tested on yours truly, and I'm living proof to their efficacy. I haven't been sick a day in the last twenty years."

Her eyes rounded in alarm. "Okay, jinx much?"

He threw his head back on a guffaw. "You're superstitious? You think I'll get deathly sick now that I've dared tempt fate?"

"Who knows? Maybe fate doesn't like braggarts."

"Actually, I think fate doesn't like gamblers." Something dark flitted across his face. Before she analyzed it, he lowered his gaze, hid it. "Since I'm anything but, I'm a good candidate for staying on its good side. For as long as possible. That brings us back to your hare tactics. Maybe you don't have loose components inside your brain to be shaken and stirred, but running like one, if you stumble, you have only one hand to ward off a fall, and you might injure it, too, or end up reinjuring your arm. And though your first trimester has been the smoothest I've ever heard about, probably as a compensation for what you're already dealing with, you *are* pregnant."

She *did* forget sometimes that she was. Not that she wanted to forget. When she did remember, it was with a burst of joy, imagining that she had a life growing inside her, that she'd have a baby to love and cherish, who'd be her flesh and blood, the family she'd never had. If there had been one thing to thank Mel for, it was that he'd somehow talked her into conceiving that baby. But because she had no symptoms whatsoever, sometimes it *did* slip her mind.

"Okay, no hare tactics." Her smile widened as she repeated his term for her jog. "But since I have no loose components, you must tell Consuelo to stop chasing me around as if I'll scatter them."

He turned his head to both sides, looked behind him. Then he turned back to her, palm over chest with an expression of mock horror. "You're talking to *me?*"

Her lips twitched. "You're the one who sicced her on me."

"A man can start a nuclear reaction, but he surely has no way of stopping it once it becomes self-perpetuating."

"You gotta call her off. She'll brush my teeth for me next!"

"You really expect me to come between her and her hurt chick? I may be lord of all I survey back at the center, but here I'm just another in the line that marches to Consuelo's tune."

"Yeah, I noticed." She chuckled, loving how he could be so alpha and capable and overriding and yet be totally comfortable letting another, and a woman, have the upper hand where she was best suited to take it. She cocked her head at him. "Families are very matriarchal here, aren't they?"

He tossed her a piece of breath-freshening gum then piled their bowls in one hand and raised the other, ring and middle fingers folded by his thumb, fore and little fingers pointing up. "Women rule."

She spluttered at the sight of him, so virile and formidable and poised, making that goofy expression and pop culture gesture.

He headed into the barbecue house and she melted back in her chair, replete and blissful. She'd never laughed like that before him. Before being here with him in his paradise of a home.

He'd only left her side to fly to work—literally, via helicopter—and had cut down on his working hours, to be there for her. She'd insisted he shouldn't, that she was perfectly all right on her own or with Consuelo, Gustavo and their children.

But she'd stopped objecting, certain he wasn't neglecting his work, had everything under control. And she couldn't get enough of being with him. Against all resolutions, she reveled in his pampering, wished with all she had in her that she could repay him in kind. But he had everything. Needed nothing. Nothing but to heal emotionally.

So she contented herself with being there for him, hoping to see him heal. And he was healing. His moroseness had dissipated and his distance had vanished, had become a closeness like she'd never known, as they discovered each other, shared so many things she'd never thought she'd share with another.

She kept waiting for him to do something to annoy her, to disappoint her, as all human beings inevitably did. But the impossible man just wouldn't. Then he went further into the realm of impossibility, kept doing things that shocked her by how much they appealed to her, delighted her.

He was everything his foster parents had said they'd picked him for and far more. Everything she admired in a human being and a man, and the most effective power for good she'd ever had the fortune to meet. And that was what he was to the world.

To her, he was all that resonated with her preferences and peculiarities. They agreed on most everything, and what they disagreed on, they discussed, came out conceding a respect for the other's viewpoint and thrilled to have gained a new awareness.

And when she added up everything he'd done for her, had been to her—her savior, protector and support—he was, yes, just incredible.

Which was why every now and then the question popped into her head—where had this man been before the accident?

From the tatters she remembered, besides his reported promiscuity, he'd treated Mel with fed-up annoyance and everyone else with abrasive impatience. His treatment of her had been the worst. He'd barely spoken to her, had watched her with something almost vicious in his eyes, as if he'd thought her beneath his friend—his brother.

And every time there was one answer. The conclusion she'd made the first day she'd come here. Her memories had to be faulty.

This, *he,* must be the truth. The magnificent truth.

"Ready to go back to your keeper?"

Everything became more beautiful with his return. She surrendered to his effortless strength, let him draw her to feet that barely touched the ground because he existed, was near.

She ended up ensconced in his protective embrace. His face clenched with the intensity she now adored, his freshness and potency filling her lungs. And it was as necessary as her next breath that she show him what he was to her.

She moved against his solid heat and power, raised her face to him, the invocation that filled her with life and hope and the will to heal, to be, trembling on her lips. "Rodrigo…"

Eight

Cybele's whisper skewered through Rodrigo, wrenching at all the emotions and responses he'd been repressing.

From every point where her body touched his, torrents of what felt like molten metal zapped through his nerves, converging to roar through his spine, jamming into his iron-hard erection.

Nothing was left in his raging depths but the need to crush her to his aching flesh, claim her, assimilate her into his being.

And he couldn't.

But how could he not—and remain sane?

Not that he was sane anymore. He hadn't been since the first time he'd laid eyes on her. And with every moment in her company, he'd been surrendering any desire to cling to sanity.

He'd plunged into the wonder of experiencing her, discovering her, sharing with her everything from his daily routines and professional pressures to his deepest beliefs and slightest whims.

And she was far more than anything he'd ever dreamed of. She was the best thing that had ever happened to him.

But whenever he was away from her, he kept dredging up the past, the suspicions and antipathies that had at once poisoned his existence and fueled his resistance. He'd *wanted* to hate and despise her, to believe the worst of her then. Because she'd been the only woman he'd ever truly wanted—and she'd been forever off-limits.

She was no longer off-limits. Not on account of Mel, nor on that of his objections to her character.

He'd moved from condemning her for tormenting Mel with her volatility to suspecting that the instability had been created in Mel's twisted psyche. Now that he was no longer jumping on anything to paint her as black as possible, and had seen all the evidence to the contrary, it made sense that a man in Mel's condition could have interpreted her acts of love—which he couldn't reciprocate in any healthy fashion—as emotional pressure and blackmail.

Later on, after their relationship had deteriorated further under the harsh realities of Mel's disability, it stood to reason that the money Mel had asked Rodrigo for to buy her things hadn't been things she'd hinted that she'd wanted. Mel had said he'd understood her demands, that she deserved some compensation to cheer her up in their endlessly trying situation.

But it could have been Mel who'd tried to satisfy any material desire of hers to placate her, to express his love in the only way he'd ever known how, and then to keep her from walking out on him in a fit of despair. And when that, too, had failed, he'd been down to the last thing he could do to prove to her that he didn't consider her his live-in nurse—give her a baby.

Rodrigo now thought her memory loss was probably her

mind's way of protecting itself from being pulverized by grief if she remembered Mel and the desperate, traumatic love she'd felt for him.

After he'd reached that conviction, he'd fluctuated between thinking she was being so wonderful to *him* because she subconsciously saw him as all she had left of Mel, to thinking she treated him as she did *because* she didn't remember loving Mel, and that when she did she'd become cold and distant again. He'd thought her coolness had been a reaction to his own barely leashed antipathy. But maybe she'd really disliked him, for reasons that were now gone with her memory. Or maybe the injury *had* caused some radical changes in her personality.

Too many maybes, too many questions the answers to which only she knew and no longer remembered. And it was driving him mad.

What if her dislike came back in full force, and this persona he adored vanished when her mind and psyche did heal completely?

The temptation to claim her now, bind her to him, negate the possibility, was too much.

He looked down in her eyes. They were fathomless with need. He could reach out and take her, and she'd be his. Ecstatically. She seemed to want him as much as he wanted her.

But did she? Or did she only think she did, because of some need to reassert her own life after surviving the accident that had claimed Mel's? Was he merely convenient, close? Or was she responding to him out of gratitude?

Whatever the reason, he didn't believe she was responsible for her desires, or capable of making a decision with so much missing from her memory.

And then there was *his* side of the story.

He had no doubt he wouldn't be betraying Mel's memory. Mel was dead, and even while he'd lived, his relationship with

Cybele had been anything but healthy or happy. If *he* could be the one to offer her that relationship, he would do anything for that chance.

But how could he live with himself if he betrayed *her* trust? And she did trust him. Implicitly. With her life. Was now showing him that she trusted him with her body, maybe her heart and future.

Yet how could he resist? Need was gnawing him hollow. And feeling her answering yearning was sending him out of his mind.

He had to plan a distraction, an intervention.

He stopped himself from cupping her face, running his fingers down her elegant nose, her sculpted cheekbones, teasing those dainty lips open, plunging his thumb inside their moistness and dampening their rose-petal softness, bending to taste her then absorbing her gasps, thrusting inside her....

He staggered away from temptation, rasped, "I have to get back to work."

She gasped at the loss of his support, bit her lip, nodded.

Coward. Work was a few hours' excuse to stay away.

He *had* to do whatever would keep him away from her until she healed and came to him with her full, unclouded, unpressured choice.

He exerted what remained of his will. "And before I forget, I wanted to tell you that I'm inviting my family for a visit."

Cybele stared up at Rodrigo.

For a moment there, as he'd held her against him, she'd thought he felt what she did, wanted what she did. She'd thought he'd take her in his arms, and she'd never be homeless again.

But it had all been in her mind. He'd torn himself away, the fierceness and the bleakness that had evaporated during the past four weeks settling back over him. She'd read him all wrong.

But he'd read her all right. There was no way he hadn't seen her desire, understood her plea for him.

And he'd recoiled from her offer, from her need, as if they'd injured him, or worse, tainted him.

But though he was too kind to castigate her for testing the limits of their situation when he'd never encouraged her to, he'd still found a way to draw the line again and keep her behind it.

He was inviting his family over. Now that she'd been so stupid as to come on to him, to offer him what he hadn't asked for and didn't want, he was making sure she'd no longer have unsupervised access to him to repeat the mistake. He was inviting them as chaperones.

That had to be his reason for suddenly thinking of inviting them. Just yesterday, they'd been talking about their families and he hadn't brought up his intention. He'd even said it would be the first year that no one came to stay at his estate at all. And she'd gotten the distinct feeling he'd been…relieved about that fact. Probably because he'd had all the distractions he could afford in the form of Mel's death and her recuperation.

But her irresponsible behavior was forcing him to put up with even more distractions than she'd caused him, through his extensive family's presence, probably until he decreed she was well enough to be let back into the wild. Which could mean weeks, maybe months.

It felt like a wake-up slap. One she'd needed. Not only couldn't she let him swamp himself with family just to keep her at arm's length, she couldn't burden him with more responsibility toward her, this time over her emotions and desires—which in his terminal nobility he was probably taking full blame for inciting. She'd burdened him enough, when she had no right to burden him at all. She had to stop leaning on him, stop taking advantage of his kindness and support. And she had to do it now, before her emotions got any deeper.

Not that she thought they could. What she felt for him filled her, overflowed.

Only one bright side to this mess. Though she'd betrayed herself and imposed on him, she was now certain she hadn't done that when Mel had been in the picture. She'd repressed her feelings before, and they must have broken free after the accident.

All she could do now was fade from his life, let him continue it free from the liability of her. She had to pick up the pieces of her life, plan how to return to a demanding job with a baby on the way, without counting on the help of a mother she was now sure wouldn't come through for her as Cybele had remembered she'd promised.

Cybele didn't need her mother. She'd long ago learned not to. And it wasn't Rodrigo's fault that she needed him emotionally. Any other kind of need had to end. Right now.

She had to leave immediately, so he wouldn't have to call his whole family to his rescue. She had to stop wasting his time, cutting into his focus and setting back his achievements.

The moment they reentered the house, she opened her mouth to say what she had to, but he talked over her.

"When I relocated here, it seemed to me that Catalans search for reasons to gather and celebrate. It was explained to me that because they've fought so fiercely to preserve their language and identity, they take extra pride in preparing and executing their celebrations. My family is thoroughly Catalan, and they're big on family unity and cultural traditions. And since I built this place over five years ago, it has replaced my grandparents' home as the place to gather. It would be a shame to interrupt the new tradition."

He was trying to make his sudden decision look as though it

had nothing to do with her snuggling up against him like a cat in heat. She wanted to cry out for him to shut up and quit being so thoughtful. She had to say her piece and he was making it so much harder. Comparing those festivities and family gatherings with the barrenness of her own life was another knife that would twist in her heart once she was away from here.

She couldn't say anything. Her throat sealed over a molten pain that filled it as he escorted her like always to her quarters, continuing her education in Catalan traditions and his family's close-knit pursuits—all the things she'd never had and would never have. "Spring and summer are rife with *fiestas i carnaval*…that means—"

"Feasts and carnivals. I know," she mumbled. "But I—"

A smile invaded his eyes and lips again, cutting her off more effectively than if he'd shouted. "I sometimes forget how good your Spanish is, and I'm blown away by how colloquial your Catalan has become in this short period."

She nearly choked on the surge of emotion and pleasure his praise provoked, only for it to be followed by an even deeper dejection.

That deepened further when he swept his gaze ahead, animation draining from his voice, the newscaster-like delivery coming back. "The closest upcoming festival is *La Diada De Sant Jordi,* or St. George's Day, celebrating the patron saint of Catalonia, on the 23rd of April. There are many variations of the legend of St. George, but the Catalan version says there was a lake that was home to a dragon to which a maiden had to be sacrificed every day. One day, St. George killed the dragon and rescued that day's maiden. A red rose tree is supposed to have grown where the dragon's blood was spilled. Now on the day, the streets of Catalonia are filled with stands selling *rosas i libros*—roses and books. The rose is a symbol of love, while the book is a symbol of culture."

"I'm sure it would be a great time to be in Catalonia—"

He bulldozed over her attempt to interrupt him. "It certainly is. The celebrations are very lively and very participatory. Anyone walking down the streets anywhere in Catalonia is invited to join. Another similar celebration is Mother of God of Montserrat, on the 27th of April. In addition to these dates, each village and town has its own designated patron saint to pay homage to. Those celebrations are much like the larger celebrations, with parades of giants made of papier-mâché, fireworks, music from live bands and more. My family may stay until the 23rd of June, which is the shortest day of the year and coincides with the summer solstice celebration and the festival honoring St. John. Here in Catalonia, we light bonfires when the sun is at its most northern point. Catalans believe this wards off disease, bad luck and assorted other demons."

She tried again. "Sounds like a fun time ahead for you and your family—"

"And for you, too. You'll love the energy and sheer fun of this time of year."

"I'm sure I would. But I won't be here for all that, so maybe another time?"

She felt his eyes turn to her then, felt their gaze as if it were his powerful arms hauling her back to him.

"What are you talking about?"

She kept walking, struggled not to give in to the need to look at him and catch his uncensored reaction to her announcement before the barrier of his surgical composure descended, obscured it. Stupid. Still wishing she mattered beyond being a duty.

"Based on your latest tests and diagnosis of my condition, and since you obviously won't do it, I'm giving myself a clean bill of health. Time to return to my life and job."

"And how do you propose to do that?" He stopped her midway in the huge sunlit corridor leading to her quarters.

"You're left-handed and can barely move your fingers. It's going to be weeks before you can do a lot of basic things for yourself, months before you can go back to work."

"Countless people with more severe and permanent disabilities are forced to fend for themselves, and they manage—"

"But you won't only be fending for yourself now. You're having a baby. And you're *not* forced to do anything—you don't have to manage on your own. I won't allow you to, and I sure as hell am not allowing you to leave. And this is the last time we have this conversation, Cybele Wilkinson."

Her heart flapped faster with each adamant word until it felt blurred like the wings of a hummingbird.

She tried to tell herself it was moronic to feel that way. That even if she had to concede that he was correct, she should listen to the voice telling her to be indignant at his overruling tactics, to rebel against his cornering her at every turn into doing what he thought was right for her. That voice also insisted there was nothing to be so giddy about, that he wasn't doing it out of concern for *her*, but for his patient.

She couldn't listen. And if another voice said she was criminally weak to be forgetting her minutes-ago resolution and clinging to whatever time she could get with him, she could only admit it. She wasn't strong enough to throw away one second she could have in his company, extensive family and all.

As for walking away for his peace of mind, she believed his acute feelings of duty wouldn't leave him any if he let her go before he judged she could handle being on her own. She also had to believe *he* could handle her being here, or he would have been relieved at her offer to leave. And since he wasn't, she shouldn't feel bad about staying. She'd offered to go, and he'd said no. Such an incredibly alpha, protective and overriding *no*.

Still, some imp inside her, which she was certain had come to life during this past month, wouldn't let her grab at his lifeline without contention. Or without trying to do what it could to erase the damage her blunder had caused to their newfound ease and rapport.

"Okay, it's clear you believe you're right—"

"I *am* right."

She went on as if he hadn't growled over her challenging opening "—but that doesn't automatically mean I agree. I came here as an alternative to staying in your center as a teaching pincushion. *But,* if I'd been there, you would have discharged me long ago. No one stays in hospital until their fractures heal."

His eyebrows descended a fraction more. "Do you enjoy futility, Cybele? We've established that when I make a decision—"

"—saying no to you isn't an option," she finished for him, a smile trembling on her lips, inviting him to smile back at her, light up the world again, tell her that he'd look past her foolish moment of weakness. "But that was a decision based on a clinical picture from a month ago. Now that I'm diagnosed as having no rattling components, I should be left to fend for myself."

She waited for him to smile back at her, decimate her argument, embroil her in another verbal tournament that neither of them wanted to win, just to prolong the match and the enjoyment.

He did neither. No smile. No decimation. He brooded down at her, seemed to be struggling with something. A decision.

Then he voiced it. "*Muy bien,* Cybele. You win. If you insist on leaving, go ahead. Leave."

Her heart plummeted down a never-ending spiral.

And he was turning around, walking away.

He'd taken no for an answer.

But he never did. He'd told her so. She'd believed him. That was why she'd said what she had.

He *couldn't* take no for an answer. That meant she'd lose him now, not later. And she couldn't lose him now. She wasn't ready to be without him for the rest of her life.

She wanted to scream that she took it all back. That she'd only been trying to do what she thought she should, assert an independence she still couldn't handle, to relieve him of the burden of her.

She didn't make a sound. She couldn't. Because her heart had splintered. Because she had no right to ask for more from him, of him. He'd given her far more than she'd thought anyone could ever give. He'd given her back her life. And it was time to give him back his, after she'd inadvertently hijacked it.

She turned away, feeling as though ice had skewered from her gut to her heart, only the freezing felt now, the pain and damage still unregistered.

Her numb hand was on her doorknob when she heard him say, "By the way, Cybele, good luck getting past Consuelo."

She staggered around. He was looking at her over his shoulder from the end of the corridor, the light from the just-below-the-ceiling windows pouring over him like a spotlight. He looked like that archangel she'd thought him before. His lips were crooked.

He was teasing her!

He didn't want her to leave, hadn't accepted that she could.

Before she could do something colossally stupid, like run and throw herself into his arms and sob her heart out, Consuelo, in a flaming red dress with a flaring skirt, swept by Rodrigo and down the corridor like a missile set on her coordinates.

She pounced on her. "You trying to undo all my work? *Seven* hours running around?" Consuelo turned and impaled Rodrigo with her displeasure. "And *you!* Letting your patient call the shots."

Rodrigo glared at her in mock-indignation before he gave Cybele a get-past-this wink. Then he turned and walked away, his bass chuckles resonating in the corridor, in her every cell.

Consuelo dragged her inside the room.

Feeling boneless with the reprieve, Cybele gave herself up to Consuelo's care, grinned as she lambasted her for her haggardness, ordered her on the scales and lamented her disappointing gains.

She'd missed out on having someone mother her. And for the time being, she'd enjoy Consuelo's mothering all she could. Along with Rodrigo's pampering and protection.

It would come to an end all too soon.

But not yet. *Not yet.*

Nine

Rodrigo stood looking down at the approaching car procession.

His family was here.

He hadn't even thought of them since the accident. He hadn't for a while before that, either. He'd had nothing on his mind but Cybele and Mel and his turmoil over them both for over a year.

He'd remembered them only when he needed their presence to keep him away from Cybele. And he'd gotten what he deserved for neglecting them for so long. They'd all had other plans.

He'd ended up begging them to come. He'd evaded explaining the reason behind his desperation. They'd probably figure it out the moment they saw him with her.

In the end, he'd gotten them to come. And made them

promise to stay. Long. He'd always wished they'd stay as long as possible.

This time he wondered if he'd survive it.

And here began his torment.

His grandparents stepped out of the limo he'd sent them, followed by three of his aunts. Out of the vans poured the aunts' adult children and their families plus a few cousins and their offspring.

Cybele stepped out of the French doors. He gritted his teeth against the violence of his response. He'd been wrestling with it for the past three days since that confrontation. He'd still almost ended up storming her bedroom every night. Her efforts to offer him sexually neutral friendliness were inflaming him far worse than if she'd been coming on to him hot and heavy.

Now she walked toward him with those energetic steps of hers, rod-straight, no wiggle anywhere, dressed in dark blue jeans and a crisp azure blouse that covered her from throat to elbows.

The way his hormones thundered, she could have been undulating toward him in stilettos, a push-up bra and a thong.

Dios. The…containment he now lived in had better be obscuring his condition.

He needed help. He needed the invasion of his family to keep him away from her door, from carrying her off to his bed.

Before she could say anything, since anything she said blinded him with an urge to plunder those mind-destroying lips, he said, "Come, let me introduce you to my tribe."

Tribe is right, Cybele thought.

She fell in step with Rodrigo as she counted thirty-eight men, women and children. More still poured from the vans. Four generations of Valderramas.

It was amazing what one marriage could end up producing.

Rodrigo had told her that his mother had been Esteban and Imelda's first child, had been only nineteen when she had him, that his grandparents had been in their early twenties when they got married. With him at thirty-eight, his grandparents must be in their late seventies or early eighties. They looked like a very good sixty. Must be the clean living Rodrigo had told her about.

She focused on his grandfather. It was uncanny, his resemblance to Rodrigo. This was what Rodrigo would look like in forty-something years' time. And it was amazingly good.

Her heart clenched on the foolish but burning wish to be around Rodrigo through all that time, to know him at that age.

She now watched as he met his family three-quarters of the way, smile and arms wide. Another wish seared her—to be the one he received with such pleasure, the one he missed that much. She envied each of those who had the right to rush to fill his arms, to be blessed by the knowledge of his vast and unconditional love. Her heart broke against the hopelessness of it all as his family took turns being clasped to his heart.

Then he turned to her, covered in kids from age two to mid-teens, his smile blazing as he beckoned to her to come be included in the boisterous affection of his family reunion.

She rushed to answer his invitation and found herself being received by his family with the same enthusiasm.

For the next eight hours, she talked and laughed nonstop, ate and drank more than she had in the last three days put together, put a name and a detailed history to each of the unpretentious, vital beings who swept her along the wave of their rowdy interaction and infectious joie de vivre.

All along she felt Rodrigo watching her even as he paid

attention to every member of his family, clearly on the best possible terms with them all. She managed not to miss one of his actions either, even as she kept up her side of the conversations. Her pleasure mounted at seeing him at such ease, surrounded by all these people who loved him as he deserved to be loved. She kept smiling at him, showing him how happy she was for him, yet trying her best not to let her longing show.

She was deep in conversation with Consuelo and two of Rodrigo's aunts, Felicidad and Benita, when he stood up, exited her field of vision. She barely stopped herself from swinging around to follow his movement. Then she felt him. At her back. His approach was like a wave of electromagnetism, sending every hair on her body standing on end, crackling along her nerves. She hoped she didn't look the way she felt, a woman in the grip of emotional and physical tumult.

His hands descended on her shoulders. Somehow she didn't lurch. "Who's letting her patient call the shots, now?"

She looked up, caught his eyebrow wiggle at Consuelo. The urge to drag him down and devour that teasing smile right off his luscious lips drilled a hole in her midsection.

The three vociferous women launched into a repartee match with him. He volleyed each of their taunts with a witticism that was more funny and inventive than the last, until they were all howling with laughter. She laughed, too, if not as heartily. She was busy having mini-heart attacks as one of his hands kept smoothing her hair and sweeping it off her shoulders absently.

By the time he bent and said, "Bed," she almost begged, *Yes, please.*

He pulled her to her feet as everyone bid her a cheerful goodnight. She insisted he didn't need to escort her to her room, that he remain with his family. She didn't think she had the strength tonight not to make a fool of herself. Again.

* * *

On *La Diada De Sant Jordi*, St. George's Day, Rodrigo's family had been there for four weeks. After the first four weeks with him, they were the second-best days of her life.

For the first time, she realized what a family was like, what being an accepted member of such a largely harmonious one could mean.

And they had more than accepted her. They'd reached out and assimilated her into their passionate-for-life, close-knit collective. The older members treated her with the same indulgence as Rodrigo, the younger ones with excitement and curiosity, loving to have someone new and interesting enter their lives. She almost couldn't remember her life before she'd met these people, before they'd made her one of their own. She didn't want to remember any time when Rodrigo hadn't filled her heart.

And he, being the magnificent human being that he was, had felt the melancholy that blunted her joy, had once again asked if her problems with her own family couldn't be healed, if he could intervene, as a neutral mediator, to bring about a reconciliation.

After she'd controlled her impulse to drown him in tears and kisses, she'd told him there hadn't exactly been a rift, no single, overwhelming episode or grievance that could be resolved. It was a lifetime of estrangement.

But the good news was—and that might be a side effect of her injuries—she was at last past the hurt of growing up the unwanted child. She'd finally come to terms with it, could finally see her mother's side of things. Though Cybele had been only six when her father had died, she'd been the difficult child of a disappointment of a husband, a constant reminder of her mother's worst years and biggest mistake. A daddy's girl who'd cried for him for years and told her mother she'd wished she'd been the one who'd died.

She could also see her stepfather's side, a man who'd found himself saddled with a dead man's hostile child as a price for having the woman he wanted, but who couldn't extend his support to tolerance or interest. They were only human, she'd finally admitted to herself, not just the grown-ups who'd neglected her. And that made it possible for her to put the past behind her.

As more good news, her mother had contacted her again, and though what she'd offered Cybele was nowhere near the unreserved allegiance Rodrigo's family shared, she wanted to be on better terms.

The relationship would never be what she wished for, but she'd decided to do her share, meet her mother halfway, take what was on offer, what was possible with her family.

Rodrigo hadn't let the subject go until he'd pressed and persisted and made sure she was really at peace with that.

She now stood looking down the beach where the children were flying kites and building sand castles. She pressed the sight between the pages of her mind, for when she was back to her monotone and animation-free life.

No. She'd never go back to that. Even when she exited Rodrigo's orbit, her baby would fill her life with—

"Do you have your book?"

She swung around to Imelda, her smile ready and wholehearted. She'd come to love the woman in that short time.

She admired Imelda's bottle-green outfit, which matched the eyes she'd passed on to Rodrigo, and was again struck by her beauty. She could barely imagine how Imelda might have looked in her prime.

Her eyes fell on the heavy volume in Imelda's hand. "What book?"

"*La Diada De Sant Jordi* is *rosas i libros* day."

"Oh, yes, Rodrigo told me."

"Men give women a red rose, and women give men a book."

Her heart skipped a beat. "Oh. I didn't know that."

"So now you know. Come on, *muchacha*, go pick a book. The men will be coming back any time now."

"Pick a book from where?"

"From Rodrigo's library, of course."

"I can't just take a book from his library."

"He'll be more than happy for you to. And then, it's what you choose that will have significance when you give it to him."

Okay. Why would Imelda suggest she give Rodrigo a book? Had she realized how Cybele felt about him and was trying to matchmake? Rodrigo hadn't been the one to betray any special emotions. He'd been no more affectionate to her than he'd been to his cousins.

Better gloss over this. "So a woman picks any man she knows, and gives him a book?"

"She can. But usually she picks the most important man in her life."

Imelda knew what Rodrigo was to her. There was certainty in her shrewd eyes, along with a don't-bother-denying-it footnote.

Cybele couldn't corroborate her belief. It would be imposing on Rodrigo. He probably knew how she felt, but it was one thing to know, another to have it declared. And then, *he* wouldn't give her a rose. Even if he did, it would be because all the women had their husbands with them for the fiesta, or because she was alone, or any other reason. She wasn't the most important woman in his life.

But after she walked back into the house with Imelda and they parted ways, she found herself rushing to the library.

She came out with the book of her choice, feeling agonizingly exposed each time one of the women passed her and commented on her having a book like them.

Then the men came back from the next town, bearing copious amounts of prepared and mouthwatering food. And each man had a red rose for his woman. Rodrigo didn't have one.

Her heart thudded with a force that almost made her sick.

She had no right to be crushed by disappointment. And no right to embarrass him. She'd give the book to Esteban.

Then she moved, and her feet took her to Rodrigo. Even if she had no claim on him, and there'd never be anything between them, he *was* the most important man in her life, and everyone knew it.

As she approached him, he watched her with that stillness and intensity that always made her almost howl with tension.

She stopped one step away, held out the book.

"Happy *La Diada De Sant Jordi*, Rodrigo."

He took the book, his eyes fixing on it, obscuring his reaction from her. She'd chosen a book about all the people who'd advanced modern medicine in the last century. He raised his eyes to her, clearly uncertain of the significance of her choice.

"Just a reminder," she whispered, "that in a collation of this century's medical giants, you'll be among them."

His eyes flared with such fierceness, it almost knocked her off her feet. Then he reached for her hand, pulled her to him. One hand clasped her back, the other traveled over her hair to cup her head. Then he enfolded her into him briefly, pressed a searing kiss on her forehead. *"Gracias mucho, querida.* It's enough for me to have your good opinion."

Next second, he let her go, turned to deliver a few festive words, starting the celebrations.

She didn't know how she functioned after that embrace. That kiss. Those words. That *querida*.

She evidently did function, even if she didn't remember anything she said or did during the next hours. Then Rodrigo was pulling her to her feet.

"Come. We're starting the Sardana, our national dance."

She flowed behind him, almost hovered as she smiled up at him, her heart jiggling at seeing him at his most carefree.

The band consisted of eleven players. They'd already taken their place at an improvised stage in the terrace garden that had been cleared for the dancers, evidently all of Rodrigo's family.

"I had the nearest town's *cobla*, our Catalan music ensemble, come over to play for us. The Sardana is never the same without live music. It's always made of four Catalan shawm players…" He pointed toward four men holding double-reed woodwinds. "Two trumpets, two horns, one trombone and a double bass."

"And what's with that guy with the flutelike instrument and the small drum attached to his left arm?"

"He plays the *flabiol*, that three-holed flute, with his left hand and plays that *tamborí* with the right. He keeps the rhythm."

"Why not just have twelve players, instead of saddling one with this convoluted setup?"

He grinned. "It's a tradition some say goes back two thousand years. But wait till you see him play. He'll make it look like the easiest thing in the world."

She grimaced down at her casted arm. "One thing's for sure, I'm not a candidate for a *flabiol/tamborí* player right now."

He put a finger below her chin, raised her face to him. "You soon will be." Before she gave in and dragged his head down to her to take that kiss she was disintegrating for, he turned his head away. "Now watch closely. They're going to dance the first *tirada,* and we'll join in the second one. The steps are very simple."

Letting out a steaming exhalation, she forced her attention to the circle of dancers that was forming.

"It's usually one man, one woman and so on, but we have more women than men here, so excuse the nontraditional configuration."

She mimicked his earlier hand gesture, drawled, "Women rule."

He threw his head back on a peal of laughter at her reminder, kept chuckling as he watched his womenfolk herding and organizing their men and children. "They do indeed."

The dance began, heated, then Rodrigo tugged her to join the *rotllanes obertes,* the open circles. They danced the steps he'd rehearsed with her on the sidelines, laughed together until their sides hurt. Everything was like a dream. A dream where she felt more alert and alive than she ever had. A dream where she was one with Rodrigo, a part of him, and in tune with the music, his family and the whole world.

Then, like every dream, the festivities drew to an end.

After calling good-night to everyone, Rodrigo walked her as usual to her quarters, left her a few steps from her door.

Two steps into the room, she froze. Her mouth fell open. Her breath left her lungs under pressure, wouldn't be retrieved.

All around. On every surface. *Everywhere.*

Red roses.

Bunches and bunches and *bunches* of perfect, bloodred roses.

Oh. God. Oh…*God…*

She darted back outside, called out to him. But he'd gone.

She stood there vibrating with the need to rush after him, find him wherever he was and smother him in kisses.

But…since he hadn't waited around for her reaction, maybe he hadn't anticipated it would be this fierce. Maybe he'd only meant to give her a nice surprise. Maybe he'd had every other woman's room filled with flowers, too. Which she wouldn't put past him. She'd never known anyone with his capacity for giving.

She staggered back into her room. The explosion of beauty and color and fragrance yanked her into its embrace again.

The need expanded, compressing her heart, her lungs.

It was no use. She had to do it. She had to go to him.

She grabbed a jacket, streaked outside.

His scent, his vibe led her to the roof.

He was standing at the waist-high stone balustrade overlooking a turbulent, after-midnight sea, a lone knight silvered by the moon, carved from the night.

She stopped a dozen steps away. He didn't turn, stood like a statue of a Titan, the only animate things his satin mane rioting around his leonine head and his clothes rustling around his steel-fleshed frame. There was no way he could have heard the staccato of her feet or the labor of her breathing over the wind's buffeting whistles. But she knew he felt her there. He was waiting for her to initiate this.

"Rodrigo." Her gasp trembled against the wind's dissipation. He turned then. Cool rays deposited glimmers in the emerald of his eyes, luster on the golden bronze of his ruggedness. She stepped closer, mesmerized by his magnificence. A step away, she reached for his hand. She wanted to take it to her lips. That hand that had saved her life, that changed the lives of countless others daily, giving them back their limbs and mobility and freeing them from pain and disability. She settled for squeezing it between both of her trembling ones. "Besides everything you've done for me, your roses are the best gift I've ever been given."

His stare roiled with his discomfort at receiving gratitude. Then he simply said, "Your book beats my roses any day."

A smile ached on her lips. "You have issues with hearing thanks, don't you?"

"Thanks are overrated."

"Nothing sincere can be rated highly enough."

"I do what I want to do, what pleases me. And I certainly never do anything expecting…anything in return."

Was he telling her that his gift wasn't hinting at any special involvement? Warning her about getting ideas?

It wouldn't change anything. She loved him with everything in her, would give him everything that she was if he'd only take it. But if he didn't want it, she *would* give him her unending appreciation. "And I thank you because I want to, because it pleases me. And I certainly don't expect you to do anything in return but accept. I accepted your thanks for the book, didn't I?"

His lips spread in one of those slow, scorching smiles of his, as if against his will. "I don't remember if I gave you a choice to accept it or not. I sort of overrode you."

"Hmm, you've got a point." Then, without warning, she tugged his hand. Surprise made him stumble the step that separated them, so that he ended up pressed against her from breast to calf. Her hand released his, went to his head, sifting through the silk of his mane, bringing it down to hers. How she wished she had the use of her other arm, so she could mimic his earlier embrace. She had to settle for pressing her longing against his forehead with lips that shook on his name.

They slid down his nose…and a cell phone rang.

He sundered their communion in a jerk, stared down at her, his eyes echoing the sea's tumult. It was shuddering, disoriented moments before her brain rebooted after the shock of interruption, of separation from him. That was her cell phone's tone.

It was in her jacket. Rodrigo had given it her, and only he had called her on it so far. Who could be calling her?

"Are you expecting a call?" His rasp scraped her nerves.

"I didn't even know anyone had this number."

"It's probably a wrong number."

"Yeah, probably. Just a sec." She fumbled the phone out, hit Answer. A woman's tear-choked voice filled her head.

"Agnes? What's wrong?" Instant anxiety gripped Rodrigo, spilled into urgency that had his hand at the phone, demanding to bear bad news himself. She blurted out the question that she hoped would defuse his agitation, "Are you and Steven okay?"

"Yes, yes…it's not that."

Cybele covered the mouthpiece, rapped her urgent assurance to Rodrigo. "They're both fine. This is something else."

His alarm drained, but tension didn't. He eased a fraction away, let her take the call, watching for any sign that necessitated his intervention, his taking over the situation.

Agnes went on. "I hate to ask you this, Cybele, but if you've remembered your life with Mel, you might know how this happened."

Foreboding closed in on her. "How *what* happened?"

"M-many people have contacted us claiming that Mel owes them extensive amounts of money. And the hospital where you used to work together says the funding he offered in return for being the head of the new general surgery department was withdrawn and the projects that were under way have incurred overdrafts in the millions. Everyone is suing us—and you—as his next of kin and inheritors."

Ten

"So you don't have any memory of those debts."

Cybele shook her head, feeling crushed by doubts and fears.

It didn't sound as if Rodrigo believed her. She had a feeling Agnes hadn't, either. Did they think Mel had incurred all those debts because of her? Worse, had he? If he had, how? Why?

Was that what Agnes had almost brought up during Mel's funeral? She'd thought Mel, in his inability to express his emotions for her any other way, had showered her with extravagant stuff? Not that she could think what could be *that* extravagant.

If that hadn't been the case, she could think of only one other way. She'd made demands of him, extensive, unreasonable ones, and he'd gone to insane lengths to meet them. But what could have forced him to do so? Threats to leave him? If that were true, then she hadn't been only a heartless monster, but a manipulative, mercenary one, too.

She had to know. She couldn't take another breath if she didn't. "Do *you* know anything about them?"

Rodrigo's frown deepened as he shook his head slowly. But his eyes were thoughtful. With suspicions? Deductions? Realizations?

"You know something. Please, tell me. I have to know."

He looked down at her for a bone-shaking moment, moonlight coasting over his beauty, throwing its dominant slashes and hollows into a conflict of light and darkness, of confusion and certainty.

Then he shook his head again, as if he'd made up his mind. To her dismay, he ignored her plea. "What I want to know is what has taken those creditors so long to come forward."

"They actually did as soon as Mel's death was confirmed."

"Then what has taken Agnes and Steven so long to relate this, and why have they come to *you* with this, and not me?"

She gave him his foster mother's explanations. "They wanted to make sure of the claims first, and then they didn't want to bother you. They thought they could take care of it themselves. They called me in case I knew something only a wife would know, that would help them resolve this mess. And because I'm involved in the lawsuits."

"Well, they were wrong, on all counts." She almost cried out at the incensed edge that entered his voice and expression. The words to beg him not to take it up with them, that they had enough to deal with, had almost shot from her lips when he exhaled forcibly. "Not that they need to know that. They've been through enough, and they were as usual misguidedly trying not to impose on me. I think those two still don't believe me when I say they *are* my parents. But anyway, none of you have anything to worry about. I'll take care of everything."

She gaped at him. *Was* he real? Could she love him more? All she could say was, "Thank you."

He squeezed his eyes on a grimace. "Don't."

"I will thank you, so live with it." He glowered at her. She went on, "And since I'm on a roll, throwing my problems in your lap, I need your opinion on another one. My arm."

His eyes narrowed. "What about it?"

"My fractures have healed, but the nerve damage isn't clearing. Eight weeks ago, you said I wouldn't be able to operate for months. Were you being overly optimistic? Will I ever regain the precision I used to have and need as a surgeon?"

"It's still early, Cybele."

"Please, Rodrigo, just give it to me straight. And before you say anything conciliatory, remember that I'll see through it."

"I would never condescend to you like that."

"Even to protect me from bad news?"

"Even then."

She believed him. He would never lie to her. He would never lie, period. So she pressed on. Needing the truth. About this, if she couldn't have it about anything else.

"Then tell me. I'm a left-handed surgeon who knows nothing else but to be one, and I need to know if in a few weeks I'll be looking to start a new career path. As you pointed out before, the arm attached to my hand had extensive nerve damage…."

"*And* I performed a meticulous peripheral nerve repair."

"Still, I have numbness and weakness, tremors—"

"It's *still* too early to predict a final prognosis. We'll start your active motion physiotherapy rehabilitation program the moment we have proof of perfect bone healing."

"We have that now."

"No, we don't. You're young and healthy and your bones *look* healed now, but I need them rock solid before I remove the cast. That won't be a day before twelve weeks after the surgery. Then we'll start your physiotherapy. We'll focus first on controlling the pain and swelling that accompanies splint removal and restoration of motion. Then we'll move to exercises to strengthen and stabilize the muscles around the wrist joint then to exercises to improve fine motor control and dexterity."

"What if none of it works? What if I regain enough motor control and dexterity to be self-sufficient but not a surgeon?"

"If that happens, you still have nothing to worry about. If worse comes to worst, I'll see to it that you change direction smoothly to whatever field of medicine will provide you with as much fulfillment. But I'm not giving up on your regaining full use of your arm and hand. I'm stopping at nothing until we get you back to normal. And don't even *think* about how long it will take, or what you'll do or where you'll be until it happens. You have all the time in the world to retrain your hand, to regain every last bit of power and control. You have a home here for as long as you wish and accept to stay. You have *me,* Cybele. *I'm* here for you, anytime, all the time, whatever happens."

And she couldn't hold back anymore.

She surged into him, tried to burrow inside him, her working arm shaking with the ferociousness of her hug. And she wept. She loved him so much, was so thankful he existed, it was agony.

He stilled, let her hug him and hold onto him and drench him in her tears. Then he wrapped her in his arms, caressed her from head to back, his lips by her ear, murmuring gentle and soothing words. Her heart expanded so quickly with a flood of love, it almost ruptured. Her tears gushed faster, her quakes nearly rattling flesh from bone.

He at last growled something as though agonized, snatched her from gravity's grasp into his, lifted her until she felt she'd float out to sea if he relinquished his hold.

He didn't, crushed her in his arms, squeezed her to his flesh until he forced every shudder and tear out of her.

Long after he'd dissipated her storm, he swayed with her, as if slow dancing the Sardana again, pressing her head into his shoulder, his other arm bearing her weight effortlessly as he raggedly swore to her in a loop of English and Catalan that he was there for her, that she'd never be without him. His movements morphed from soothing to inflaming to excruciating. But it was his promises that wrenched at the tethers of her heart.

For she knew he would honor every promise. He would remain in her life and that of her baby's. As the protector, the benefactor, the dutiful, doting uncle. And every time she saw him or heard from him it would pour fresh desperation on the desolation of loving him and never being able to have him.

She had to get away. Today. Now. Her mind was disintegrating, and she couldn't risk causing herself a deeper injury. Her baby needed her healthy and whole.

"Cybele…" He shifted his grip on her, and his hardness dug into her thigh.

She groped for air, arousal thundering through her. Voices inside her yelled that this was just a male reaction to having a female writhing in his arms, that it meant nothing.

She couldn't listen. It didn't matter. He was aroused. This could be her only chance to be with him. And she had to take it. She needed the memory, the knowledge that she'd shared her body with him to see her through the barrenness of a life without him.

She rubbed her face into his neck, opened her lips on his pulse. It bounded against her tongue, as if trying to drive deeper into her mouth, mate with her. Every steel muscle she was wrapped around expanded, bunched, buzzed. She whimpered at the feel of his flesh beneath her lips, the texture, the taste, at the sheer delight of breathing him in, absorbing his potency.

"Cybele, *querida*…" He began to put her down and she clung, captured his lips before he said any more, before he could tell her no.

She couldn't take no for an answer. Not this time. She had to have this time.

She caught his groans on her tongue, licked his lips of every breath, suckled his depths dry of every sound. She arched into his arousal, confessing hers without words. Then with them.

"Rodrigo—I *want* you." That came out a torn sob. "If you want me, *please*—just take me. Don't hold back. Don't think. Don't worry. No consequences or considerations. No tomorrows."

Rodrigo surrendered to Cybele, let her take of him what she would, his response so vast it was like a hurricane building momentum before it unleashed its destruction.

But her tremulous words replayed in his mind as she rained petal softness and fragrant warmth all over his face, crooning and whimpering her pleas for his response, her offer of herself. He felt things burning inside him as he held back, the significance of her words expanding in his mind.

Carte blanche. That was what she was giving him. With her body, with herself. No strings. No promises. No expectations.

Because she didn't want any? Because her need was only sexual? Or because she couldn't handle more than that? But what if she couldn't handle *even* that? If he gave her what she thought she wanted and ended up damaging her more?

And though he was nearly mindless now, powerless against the force of her desire, he'd conditioned himself to protect her from his own. "Cybele, you're distraught—"

She sealed his lips again, stopping his objection, her tongue begging entry, her kisses growing fevered, singeing the last of his control. "With need for you. I sometimes feel it will shatter me. I know what I'm asking. Please, Rodrigo, please…just give me this time."

This time. She thought he could stop at once, that he could possess her then walk away? It wasn't carte blanche, just a one-time offer? Would all that need she talked about then be quenched? Did she not feel more for him because her emotions had been buried with Mel, even if she didn't remember?

That thought gave him the strength to put her down, step out of reach when she stumbled to embrace him again.

Her arms fell to her sides, her shoulders hunching as she suddenly looked fragile and lost.

Then her tears flowed again, so thick it seemed they shriveled up her face. "Oh, no—y-you already showed me that you don't want me, and I—I came on to you again…."

She choked up, stumbled around and disappeared from the roof.

He should let her go. Talk to her again when his body wasn't pummeling him in demand for hers. But even if he could survive his own disappointment, he couldn't survive hers. He couldn't let her think he didn't want her. He had to show her the truth, even if the price was having her only once. He would take anything he could have of her, give her anything she needed.

He tore after her, burst into her room, found her crumpled facedown on her bed, good arm thrown over one of the bouquets he'd flooded her room with. She lurched at his entry, half-twisted to watch his approach, her wet gaze wounded and wary.

He came down on his knees at the foot of the bed. Her smooth legs, which had tanned honey-colored under his agonized eyes these past weeks, were exposed as the long, traditionally Catalan red skirt he'd picked for her to wear today rode up above her knees.

He wanted to drag her to him, slam her into his flesh, overpower and invade her, brand her, devour her whole.

He wanted to cherish her, savor and pleasure her more.

She gasped as he slipped off her shoes, tried to turn to him fully. He stopped her with a gentle hand at the small of her back. She subsided with a whimpering exhalation, watched him with her lip caught in her teeth as he prowled on all fours, advancing over her, kissing and suckling his way from the soles of her feet, up her legs, her thighs, her buttocks and back, her nape. She lay beneath him, quaking and moaning at each touch until he traced the lines of her shuddering profile. The moment he reached her lips, she cried out, twisted onto her back, surged up to cling to his lips in a desperate, soul-wrenching kiss.

Without severing their meld, he scooped her up and stepped off the bed. She relinquished his lips on a gasp of surprise.

"I want you in my bed, *querida*."

She moaned, shook her head. "No, please." He jerked in alarm. She didn't want to be in his bed? He started to put her down when she buried her face and lips in his neck. "Here. Among the roses."

"Dios, si…"

He'd fantasized about having her in his bed from the day he'd first laid eyes on her. Even when she'd become a forbidden fantasy, her image, and the visualization of all the things he'd burned to do to her, with her, even when he'd hated her and himself and the whole world for it, had been what had fueled his self-pleasuring, providing the only relief he'd had.

He'd covered his bed with the royal blue of her eyes. The rest of the room echoed the mahogany of her hair and the honey of her skin. He'd needed to sleep surrounded by her.

But this was far better than his fantasies. To have her here, among the blazing-red beauty of his blatant confession that she was his most important woman. His most important person.

He hadn't meant to confess it, but couldn't stop himself. He also hadn't dreamed it would lead to this. To beyond his dreams.

He laid her back on the bed, stood back taking her in. Unique, a ravishing human rose, her beauty eclipsing that of the flowers he'd filled her room with. She must have realized their significance, encouraging her to divulge her own need.

He felt his clothes dissolve off his body under the pressure of his own, under her wide-eyed awe, her breathless encouragement.

Then he was all over her again, caressing her elastic-waist skirt from her silky legs, kneading her jacket off, then the ensemble blouse over her head. Her bra and panties followed as he traced the tide of peach flooding her from toes to cheeks, tasting each tremor strumming her every fiber.

Then he was looking down on what no fantasy had conjured. Thankfully. Or he would have lost his mind for real long ago.

He remained above her, arms surrounding her head, thighs imprisoning hers, vibrating as the sight, the scent and sounds of her surrender pulverized his intentions to be infinitely slow and gentle. Blood thundered in his head, in his loins, tearing the last tatters of control from his grasp in a riptide.

Then she took it all out of his hands, her hand trembling over his back in entreaty, its power absolute.

He surrendered, moved between her shaking thighs, pressed her shuddering breasts beneath his aching chest. Then she conquered him, irrevocably.

Her lips trembled on his forehead, his name a litany of tremulous passion and longing as she enveloped him, clasped him to her body as if her life depended on his existence, his closeness, on knowing he was there, as if she couldn't believe he was.

Tenderness swamped him, choked him. He had to show her, prove to her, that he was there, was hers. He'd already given her all he had. All he had left to give her was his passion, his body.

He rose on his knees, cupped her head in one hand, her buttocks in the other, tilted one for his kiss, the other for his penetration. He bathed the head of his erection in her welcoming wetness, absorbed her cries of pleasure at the first contact of their intimate flesh, drank her pleas to take her, fill her.

He succumbed to the mercilessness of her need and his, drew back to watch her eyes as he started to drive into her, to join them. Her flesh fluttered around his advance, hot and tight almost beyond endurance, seeming to drag him inside and trying to push him out at once, begging for his invasion while resisting it.

He tried again and again, until she was writhing beneath him, eyes streaming, her whole body shaking and stained in the flush of uncontrollable arousal and unbearable frustration.

His mind filled with confusion and colliding diagnoses.

"Please, just do it, Rodrigo, hard, just take me."

The agony in her sobs was the last straw. He had to give her what she needed, couldn't draw his next breath if he didn't.

He thrust past her resistance, buried half of his shaft inside her rigid tightness.

It was only when her shriek tore through him that he understood what was that ripping sensation he'd felt as he'd driven into her. And he no longer understood anything.

It was impossible. Incomprehensible.

She was a *virgin?*

Eleven

Rodrigo froze on top of Cybele, half-buried in her depths, paralyzed. A virgin? *How?*

He raised himself on shaking arms. Her face contorted and a hot cry burst from her lips. He froze in midmotion, his gaze pinned on hers as he watched her eyes flood with the same confusion, the same shock along with tears.

"It shouldn't hurt that much, should it?" she quavered. "I couldn't have forgotten *that*."

Dios. He'd wanted to give her nothing but pleasure and more pleasure. And all he'd done was *hurt* her.

"No" was all he could choke out.

She digested that, reaching the same seemingly impossible explanation he had. "Then you have to be…my first."

Her first. The way she said that, with such shy wonder, made him want to thrust inside her and growl, *And your only*.

Something far outside his wrecked restraint—probably

the debilitating cocktail of shock and shame at causing her pain—held him back from that mindless display of caveman possessiveness.

"I remember I wanted to wait until, y'know, I met…the one. I assumed that when I met Mel… But it—it seems I wanted to wait until we were married. But…"

He'd been trying to get himself to deflate, enough to slip out of her without causing her further pain. He expanded beyond anything he'd ever known instead. His mind's eye crowded with images of him devouring those lips that quivered out her earnest words, those breasts that swelled with her erratic breathing.

"But since there are ways for paraplegics to have sex, I still assumed we did one way or…" She choked with embarrassment. It was painfully endearing, when their bodies were joined in ultimate intimacy. "But it's clear we didn't, at least nothing invasive, and artificial insemination is essentially noninvasive…."

He shouldn't find her efforts at a logical, medically sound analysis that arousing as she lay beneath him, shaking, her impossible tightness throbbing around his shaft, her torn flesh singeing his own. But—curse him—it was arousing him to madness. He wanted to *give* her invasive.

He couldn't. He had to give her time, for the pain that gripped her body to subside. He started to withdraw. Her sob tore through him.

He froze, his own moan mingling with hers until she subsided. Then he tried to move again. But she clamped quaking legs around his hips, stopping him from exiting her body, pumping her own hips, impaling herself further on his erection.

"I'm hurting you." He barely recognized the butchered protest that cracked the panting-filled silence as his.

"Yes, oh, *yes*…" He heaved up in horror. She clung harder, her core clamping him like a fist of molten metal. "It's…

exquisite. You are. I dreamed—but could have never dreamed how you'd feel inside me. You're burning me, filling me, making me feel—feel so—so—oh, Rodrigo, take me, do everything to me."

He roared with the spike of arousal her words lashed through him. Then, helpless to do anything but her bidding, he thrust back into her, shaking with the effort to be gentle, go slow. She thrashed her head against the sheets, splashing her satin tresses, bucking her hips beneath his, engulfing more of his near-bursting erection into her heat. "*Don't.* Give me…all of you, do it…hard."

He growled his capitulation as he rose, cupped her hips in his palms, tilted her and thrust himself to the hilt inside her.

At her feverish cry, he withdrew all the way, looked down at the awesome sight of his shaft sinking slowly inside her again.

He raised his eyes to hers, found her propped up on her elbows, watching too, lips crimson, swollen, open on frantic pants, eyes stunned, wet, stormy. He drew out, plunged again, and she collapsed back, crying out a gust of passion, opening wider for each thrust, a fusion of pain and pleasure slashing across her face, rippling through her body.

He kept his pace gentle, massaging her all over with his hands, his body, his mouth, bending to suckle her breasts, drain her lips, rain wonder all over her.

"Do you know what you are? *Usted es divina, mi belleza, divina.* Do you see what you do to me? What I'm doing to you?"

She writhed beneath him with every word, her hair rippling waves of copper-streaked gloss over the crisp white sheet, her breathing fevered, her whole body straining at him, around him, forcing him to pick up speed—though he managed not to give in to his body's uproar for more force.

"I *love* what you're doing to me—your flesh in mine—give it to me—give it all to me…."

He again obeyed, strengthened his thrusts until her depths started to ripple around him and she keened, bucked up, froze, then convulsion after convulsion squeezed soft shrieks out of her, squeezed her around his erection in wrenching spasms.

The force, the sight and sound and knowledge of her release smashed the last of his restraint. He roared, let go, his body all but detonating in ecstasy. His hips convulsed into hers and he felt his essence flow into her as he fed her pleasure to the last tremor, until her arm and legs fell off him in satiation.

He collapsed beside her, shaking with the aftershocks of his life's most violent and first profound orgasm, moved her over him with extreme care, careful to remain inside her.

She spread over him, limp, trembling and cooling. He'd never known physical intimacy could be like this, channeling into his spirit, his reason. It had been merciful he hadn't imagined how sublime making love to her would be. He *would* have long ago gone mad.

He encompassed her velvet firmness in caresses, letting the sensations replay in his mind and body, letting awe overtake him.

He was her first. And she'd needed him so much that even through her pain, she'd felt so much pleasure at their joining.

Not that it had mattered to him in any way when he'd thought she'd belonged to Mel, had probably been experienced before him.

But now he knew she'd been with no one else, he almost burst with pride and elation. She *was* meant to be his alone.

And he had to tell her that he was hers, too. He had to offer her. Everything. *Now.*

"Cybele, *mi corazón*," he murmured into her hair as he

pressed her into his body, satiation, gratitude and love swamping him. *"Cásate conmigo, querida."*

Cybele lay draped over Rodrigo, shell-shocked by the transfiguring experience.

Every nerve crackled with Rodrigo-induced soreness and satiation and a profundity of bliss, amazement and disbelief.

She'd been a virgin. Wow.

And what he'd done to her. A few million wows.

The wows in fact rivaled the number of his billions since he'd given her all that pleasure when she'd simultaneously been writhing with the pain of his possession. But the very concept of having him inside her body, of being joined to him in such intimacy, at last, had swamped the pain, turned it into pleasure so excruciating she thought she *had* died in his arms for moments there.

Love welled inside her as she recalled him looking down at her in such adorable contrition and stupefaction. The latter must have been because she'd babbled justifications for her virginal state with him buried inside her. Another breaker of heat crashed over her as she relived her mortification. Then the heat changed texture when she recalled every second of his domination.

What would he do to her when pain was no longer part of the equation? When he no longer feared hurting her? When he lost the last shred of inhibition and just plundered her?

She wondered if she'd survive such pleasure. And she couldn't wait to risk her life at the altar of his unbridled possession.

She was about to attempt to beg for more, needing to cram all she could into her one time in his arms. But she lost coherence as he caressed and crooned to her. Then his words registered.

Cásate conmigo, querida.

Marry me, darling.

Instinctive responses and emotions mushroomed, paralyzed her, muted her. Heart and mind ceased, time and existence froze.

Then everything rushed, streaked. Elation, disbelief, joy, shock, delight, doubt. The madly spinning roulette of emotions slowed down, and one flopped into the pocket. Distress.

She pushed away from the meld of their bodies, moaning at the burn of separation, rediscovering coordination from scratch. "I meant it when I said no tomorrows, Rodrigo. I don't expect anything."

He rose slowly to a sitting position, his masculinity taking on a harsher, more overwhelming edge among the dreamy softness of a background drenched in red roses. He looked like that wrathful god she'd seen in the beginning, decadent in beauty, uncaring of the effect his nakedness and the sight of his intact arousal had on flimsy mortals like her. "And you don't want it, either?"

"What I want isn't important."

He stopped her as she turned away, his grip on her arm gentleness itself, belying his intensity as he gritted, "It's *all*-important. And we've just established how much you want me."

"It still makes no difference. I—I can't marry you."

He went still. "Because of Mel? You feel guilty over him?"

She huffed a bitter laugh. "And you don't?"

"No, I don't," he shot back, adamant, final. "Mel is no longer here and this has nothing to do with him."

"Says the man whose every action for the last ten weeks had everything to do with Mel."

He rose to his knees, blocked her unsteady attempt to get off the bed. "Care to explain that?"

Air disappeared as his size dwarfed her, his heat bore down

on her, as his erection burned into her waist. She wanted to throw herself down, beg him to forget about his honor-bound offer and just ride her to oblivion again.

She swallowed fire past her hoarse-with-shrieks-of-pleasure vocal cords. "I'm Mel's widow, and I'm carrying his unborn child. Need more clues?"

"You think all I did for you was out of duty for him?"

She shrugged dejectedly. "Duty, responsibility, dependability, heroism, nobility, honor. You're full of 'em."

And he did the last thing she'd expected in this tension.

He belted out one of those laughs that turned her to boiling goo. "You make it sound like I'm full of…it."

Words squeezed past the heart bobbing in her throat. "I wish. You make it impossible to think the least negative thing of you."

He encroached on her as he again exposed her to that last thing she'd thought she'd ever see from him. Pure seduction, lazy and indulgent and annihilating. "And that's bad…why?"

Oh, *no*. She'd been in deep…it, when he'd been only lovely and friendly. Now, after he'd kick-started her sexuality software with such an explosive demonstration, had imprinted his code and password all over her cells, to all of a sudden see fit to turn on his sex appeal intentionally was cruel and unusual overkill.

She tried to put a breath between them. He wouldn't let her, backed her across the bed, a panther crowding his prey into a corner. She came up against the brass bars, grabbed them, tried to pull up from her swooning position.

"It's bad because it makes it impossible to say no to you."

His lips twitched as he prowled over her, imprisoning her in a cage of muscle and maleness. But instead of his previous solemn and tender intensity, that mind-messing predatory sexiness spiked to a whole new level. "That has always been my nefarious plan."

"Okay, Rodrigo, I'm confused here," she panted. "What's brought all...*this* about?"

His eyebrows shot up in mock-surprise and affront. "You mean you don't remember? Seems I have to try much...harder—and longer—to make a more lasting impression."

She coughed in disbelief. "You're telling me you suddenly want to marry me because of the mind-blowing pleasure?"

He tightened his knees around her thighs, winding the pounding between them into a tighter rhythm, licking his lips as his gaze melted over her captive nakedness, making her feel as if he'd licked her all over again. "So it was mind-blowing for you?"

"Are you kidding? I'm surprised my head is still screwed on. But I can't believe it was for *you*. I'm not by any stretch hot stuff, not to mention I must have cramped your style, being your first pregnant virgin and all."

"I admit, I was and am still agonizingly cramped, as you can see. And feel." He pressed his erection into her belly. Feeling the marble smooth and hard column of hot flesh against hers, the awe that she'd accommodated all that inside her, the carnality of the sharply recalled sensations as he'd occupied her, stretched her into mindlessness made her gasp, arch up involuntarily into his hardness. He ground harder into her as he drove a knee between her thighs, coaxing their rigidity to melt apart for him. "And in case you want to know my style..." His other knee joined in splaying her thighs apart as he leaned over her, teasing her aching nipples with the silk-sprinkled power of his chest. "...it's a woman who has no idea she's inferno-level stuff who happens to be a pregnant virgin. Or who was one, until I put an end to that condition."

She couldn't wrap her head around this. "So if it isn't out of duty to Mel, it isn't something more moronically honorable as doing the 'right thing' since you took my 'innocence,' is it?"

He chuckled. "*Dios,* you say the funniest things. First, I don't equate virginity with innocence. Second, *your* innocence seems to be almost intact. But don't worry. I didn't even scratch the surface of all the ways I plan to rectify that." He nipped her nipple, had her coming off the bed with a sharp slam of pleasure. He withdrew on a sigh of satisfaction. "Any more far-fetched reasons you can come up with to explain why I'm proposing to you?"

"Why don't you tell me your not-so-far-fetched ones?" she gasped. "And don't say because I'm your one and only aphrodisiac. That wasn't the case up until a few hours ago."

"Up until a few hours ago, I didn't know you wanted me."

"That's as straight-faced a lie as I've ever heard," she scoffed. "I'm as transparent as the windows Consuelo keeps spotless. I showed you I wanted you weeks ago. Hell, I showed you I wanted you two minutes after I regained consciousness."

He tasted her nipples in soft pulls as if compelled. "That you did so soon, coupled with your loss of memory, made me wonder if your mind wasn't scrambled and you didn't know what you wanted, or why. I thought I might be what you clung to, to reaffirm your life after surviving such a catastrophe, or because I was the one closest to you, or the one you seemed to perceive as your savior."

She pushed his head away before her breasts—her whole body—exploded. "You *are* my savior, but that has nothing to do with my wanting you." She devoured his beauty as he loomed over her, felt her core clench with the memory, the knowledge of what he could do to it. "I remember you had hordes of women you didn't save panting for you. I think *not* wanting you is a feminine impossibility."

The intimacy and seduction on his face turned off like a

light, plunging her world into darkness. "So it's only sexual for you? That's why you wanted it to be only once?"

"Which part of me lauding your responsibility, dependability, heroism, nobility and honor didn't you get?"

The mesmerizing heat flared back on like floodlights, making her squirm. "So you like me for my character not just my body?"

"I *love* you for your character." That made that smug, male assurance falter, crack. He stared at her, stunned, almost vulnerable. She groaned. "I didn't intend to say that, so don't go all noble pain-in-the-derriere on me and find it more reason to—"

He crashed his lips onto hers, silencing her, wrenching keens from her depths on scorching, devouring kisses. He came fully over her body, grinding into her belly, lifting her off the bed, one hand supporting her head for his ravaging, the other at her back holding her for his chest to torment her breasts into a frenzy.

She tore her lips away before she combusted and it was too late to vent her reservations. "Please, Rodrigo, don't feel you owe me anything. And I can't owe you any more than I already do."

He plastered her back to the bed, seemingly by the force of his conviction alone. "You owe me nothing, do you hear? It's been my privilege to see to your health, my joy to have you in my home, and yes, my mind-blowing pleasure to have you in my bed."

She started shaking again. It was too much. Loving him, needing to grab at him, to take him at his every magnificent word, blocking her mind to the fear that she'd be taking advantage of him, end up causing them both misery and heartache.

She trembled caresses over his beloved face. "I know you're always right, but you're totally wrong here. I owe you far more than medical care and shelter. And mind-blowing pleasure. I owe you for restoring my faith in humanity, for showing me what a family could be like, and letting me be a part of yours for a while, for stabilizing my outlook so much that I feel I will at last have a relationship with my own family, not just cynical and bitter avoidance. I owe you memories and experiences that have made me a stronger, healthier person, that will be a part of me forever. And that was before what you offered me today."

He grabbed her hand, singed it in kisses, all lightness burned away as he, too, vibrated with emotion. "Mel's debts…"

She rushed to make one thing clear. "I don't know what hand I had in them, but if I had any, I'll pay my part, I swear."

"No, you won't. I said I'd take care of them."

"You'd do anything to protect your foster parents, and me, too, won't you? And *this* is what I'm indebted to you for. The—the… carte blanche support. And you're offering it forever now. And I can't accept. I can't burden you anymore with my problems. Any more support from you would burden *me*. Whatever your reasons are for offering to marry me, I have nothing to offer you in return."

His hands convulsed in her hair, pinned her for the full impact of his vehemence. "You have everything to offer me, *querida*. You've *already* offered me everything and I want it all for the rest of my life. I want your passion, your friendship, and now that I know I have it, I want your love. I *need* your love. And I want your baby as mine. I want us to be lovers, to be a family. And the only reason I want all this is because I love you."

She lurched so hard she nearly threw him off her. He pressed down harder, holding her head tighter to imprint her with every nuance of his confession. "I love you, *mi amor,* for your character and your body, for being such a responsible, dependable, heroic, noble and honorable pregnant has-been-virgin who had no idea you started a fire in me that can never be put out."

She broke into sobs. "How can you say that? I was going to leave, and if I hadn't almost attacked you, you would have never—"

"I would have *never* let you leave. Don't you get that yet? I was going to keep shooting down your reasons and demands to leave for months to come, and when I was out of arguments, I was going to make you offers you can't refuse so you'd have to stay. I would have confessed my feelings to you when I felt secure you could make such a life-changing decision and lifelong commitment, could handle my feelings and my passion. You only freed me from the agonizing wait. Thankfully. I was suffering serious damage holding back."

Her tears slowed down with each incredible word out of that mouth that sent her to heaven no matter what it did or said. Scary joy and certainty started to banish the agony of grief and doubt.

"You hid that perfectly," she hiccuped, her face trembling, with a smile of burgeoning belief in his reciprocated emotions.

His sincerity and intensity switched to bedevilment in a flash as his hands and lips started to roam her again. "I'm a neurosurgeon. Covert turmoil is one of my middle names."

"Another one?" She spluttered on mirth and emotion, finally felt she had the right to reciprocate his caresses, delighting in the silk of his polished, muscled back and swimmer's shoulders.

But she had to voice her concerns one last time. "This is a major step. Are you sure you considered all the ramifications?"

"The only thing that stopped me from snatching you up the first time you offered yourself was that I thought *you* were nowhere near aware of the ramifications, had no idea what you'd be letting yourself in for, weren't ready for a relationship so soon after such a loss and trauma. I, on the other hand, am positive of what I want. What I *have* to have. You, the baby. *Us*."

She cried out and dragged him down to her, surging up to meet his lips, devouring with her own. She was begging when he suddenly rose, swept her up in his arms and strode into her bathroom.

He put her down on the massage table and ran a bubble bath, came back to slide her off it, locking her thighs around his hips, gliding his erection along her core's molten lips before he leaned forward, pressed it to her belly, undulated against her, filled her gasping mouth with his tongue.

She arched, tried to bring him inside her. He held her down, wouldn't let her have what she felt she was imploding for.

"You haven't said yes."

"I've been saying 'yes...but' for a while now," she moaned.

"Didn't sound like that to me."

"Is that why you're punishing me now?"

"I would be punishing you if I gave you what you think you want again tonight. But don't worry, there are so many other ways I'll go about erasing that innocence of yours."

"No, please...I want you again."

"Let me hear that *yes* without the *but* and you can have me. For the rest of our lives."

"*Yes*."

And for the rest of the night, she lost count of how many *yeses* she said.

Twelve

Three months and a half to the day that Cybele opened her eyes in Rodrigo's world, she was trying not to run down the aisle to him.

She rushed down the path between their guests, his family and friends and colleagues, in one of the plateau gardens overlooking his vineyards on one side and the sea on the other, feeling like she was treading air, forging deeper into heaven.

He'd insisted on scheduling the wedding two weeks after he'd removed her cast, to give time for the physiotherapy to control any lingering discomforts. But he hadn't insisted on holding the wedding in Barcelona's biggest cathedral as he'd first planned, succumbing to her desire to hold it on his estate. The land that was now theirs. Their home. And their baby's home.

That was what completed her happiness. That it wasn't only she who was being blessed by the best gift the world had to offer, but her baby, too. Only Rodrigo would love as his own the baby of the man he'd loved like a brother.

He stood there looking godlike in his tuxedo, his smile growing more intimate and delighted as she neared him. She only noticed Ramón standing beside him when she stumbled the last steps to grab Rodrigo's outstretched hand. She absently thought that they could be brothers. Not that Ramón, who was arguably as esthetically blessed as Rodrigo, was anywhere near as hard-hitting. Or perhaps it was she who had terminal one-man-one-woman syndrome.

Ramón winked at her as he kissed her and left them to the minister's ministrations. He'd come to her quarters an hour ago, where Rodrigo had insisted she remain until their wedding night, and performed the Catalan best man's duty of giving the bride her bouquet, which he'd picked for her, while reciting a poem he'd written. She'd almost had a heart attack laughing as he turned the poem that was supposed to extol her virtues and that of her groom into a hilariously wicked medical report.

Apart from that, and standing by Rodrigo's side until she reached him, Ramón's role had ended. In Catalonia there were no wedding rings for the best man to bear. Rodrigo would transfer the engagement ring from her right hand to her left one.

He was doing that now. She barely remembered the preceding ritual beyond repeating the vows, crying a river as Rodrigo made his own vows to her, lost in his eyes, singed by his love.

She watched their hands entwine as he slipped the ring onto her trembling finger, the ten-carat blue diamond part of the set she was wearing that totaled a breath-depleting fifty carats. He'd said he'd picked them for being a lighter version of her eyes.

Then he kissed her. As if they were now one. Forever.

From then on, everything blurred even more as their guests

carried them away to another extensive session of Sardana dances and many other wedding customs and festivities.

At one point she thought she'd had a brief exchange with Mel's parents. She had the impression that they were doing much better and seemed genuinely happy for her and Rodrigo. Her family was here, too, flown in by Rodrigo. His magic had encompassed them, as well, had infused them with a warmth they'd never exhibited before.

Then the dreamlike wedding was over and he carried her to his quarters. Theirs now. At last.

She'd almost lost her mind with craving these past weeks, as she hadn't slept curved into his body, or taken him inside of hers.

She was in a serious state by now. She'd die if he took her slowly and gently like he'd done that first night.

She was about to beg him not to when he set her down, pressed her against the door and crashed his lips onto hers.

She cried out her welcome and relief at his fierceness, surrendered to his surging tongue. His hands were all over her as he plundered her mouth, removing the *peineta* and pins that held her cutwork lace veil in place, shaking her hair out of the imprisonment of her Spanish chignon, undoing the string lacing of her traditional wedding gown's front.

He pushed it off her shoulders, spilling her breasts into his palms, weighing and kneading them until she felt they would burst if he didn't devour them. He was looking down at them as if he really would. Then he crushed them beneath his chest, her lips beneath his, rubbing, thrusting, maddening.

"Do you have any idea how much I've hungered for you?" he groaned against her lips. "What these past weeks were like?"

"If it's half as much as I hungered for you, and they were half as excruciating as mine, then…serves you right."

He grunted a sound so carnal and predatory yet amused,

sowed a chain of nips from her lips to her nipples in chastisement as he dragged her dress down. It snagged on her hips.

He reversed his efforts, tried to get it over her head, and she hissed, "Rip it."

His eyes widened. Then with a growl, he ripped the white satin in two. She lurched and moaned, relishing his ferocity, fueling it.

He swept her underwear down her legs, then stood to fling away his jacket, cummerbund and tie then gave her a violent strip-show shredding of his shirt. Candlelight cast a hypnotic glow to accompany his performance. Passion rose from her depths at the savage poetry of his every straining muscle. To her disappointment, he kept his pants on.

Before she could beg him to complete his show, he came down before her, buried his face in her flesh, in her core, muttered love and lust. When she was begging for him, he rose with her wrapped around him, took her to bed, laid her on her back on its edge, kneeled between her thighs, probed her with deft fingers.

He growled his satisfaction as her slick flesh gripped them. "Do you know what it does to me—to feel you like this, to have this privilege, this freedom? Do you know what it means to me, that you let me, that you want me, that you're mine?"

Sensation rocketed, more at the emotion and passion fueling his words than at his expert pleasuring. She keened, opened herself fully to him, now willing to accept pleasure any way he gave it, knowing he craved her surrender, her pleasure. She'd always give him all he wanted.

He came over her, thrust his tongue inside her mouth to the rhythm of his invading fingers, his thumb grinding her bud in escalating circles. He swallowed every whimper, every tremulous word, every tear, until she shuddered apart in his arms.

She collapsed, nerveless and sated. For about two minutes.

Then she was all over him, kissing, licking, nipping and kneading him through his pants. He rasped, "Release me."

She lowered the zipper with shaking hands. Her mouth watered as he sprang heavy and hard into her palms. He groaned in a bass voice that spilled magma from her core, "Play with me, *mi amor*. Own me. I'm yours."

"And do you know what hearing you say this means to me?" she groaned back.

He growled as her hands traveled up and down his shaft, pumping his potency in delight. She slithered down his body, tasted him down to his hot, smooth crown. His scent, taste and texture made her shudder with need for all of him. She spread her lips over him, took all she could of him inside. He grunted his ecstasy, thrust his mighty hips to her suckling rhythm.

His hand in her hair stopped her. "I need to be inside you."

She clambered over him, kissing her way to his lips, "And I need you inside me. Don't you dare go slow or gentle… *please…*"

With that last plea, she found herself on her back beneath him, impaled, filled beyond capacity, complete, the pleasure of his occupation insupportable.

"Cybele, *mi amor, mi vida*," he breathed into her mouth, as he gave her what she'd been disintegrating for, with the exact force and pace that had her thrashing in pleasure, driving deeper and deeper into her, until he nudged her womb.

Her world imploded into a pinpoint of shearing sensation, then exploded in one detonation after another of bone-rattling pleasure. He fed her convulsions, slamming into her, pumping her to the last abrading twitches of fulfillment.

Then he surrendered to his own climax, and the sight and sound of him reaching completion inside her, the feel of his body shuddering over hers with the force of the pleasure he'd found inside her, his seed jetting into her core, filling her to overflowing, had her in the throes of another orgasm until she was weeping, the world receding as pleasure overloaded her.

She came to, to Rodrigo kissing her, worry roughening his voice. "Cybele, *mi alma, por favor,* open your eyes."

Her lids weighed tons, but she opened them to allay his anxiety. "I thought you knocked me senseless the first time because it *was* the first time. Seems it's going to be the norm. Not that you'll hear anything but cries for an encore from this end."

She felt the tension drain from his body, pour into the erection still buried inside her. His gaze probed her tear-drenched face, proprietary satisfaction replacing the agitation in eyes that gleamed with that Catalan imperiousness. "In that case, prepare to spend half of our married life knocked senseless."

She giggled as he wrapped her nerveless body around him and prowled to the bathroom. He took her into the tub, already filled, laid her between his thighs, her back to his front, supporting her as she half floated. He moved water over her satiated body, massaging her with it as he did with his legs and lips. She hummed with the bliss reverberating in her bones.

She would have taken once with him, would have lived on the memory forever. But this *was* forever. It was so unbelievable that sometimes she woke up feeling as if she were suffocating, believing that it had all been a delusion.

She had serious security issues. This perfection was making her more scared something would happen to shatter it all.

He sighed in contentment. *"Mi amor milagrosa."*

She turned her face into his chest, was about to whisper back that it was he who was the miracle lover when a ring sounded from the bedroom. The center calling.

He exhaled a rough breath. "They've *got* to be kidding."

She turned in his arms. "It has to be something major,

if they're calling you on your wedding night. You have to answer."

He harrumphed as he rose, dried himself haphazardly and went to answer. He came back frowning. "Pile up, serious injuries. Son and wife of an old friend among them." He drove his fingers in his hair. "*¡Maldita sea!* I only started making love to you."

"Hey. Surgeon here, too, remember? Nature of the beast." She left the tub, dried quickly, hugged him with both arms—an incredible sensation. "And you don't have to leave me behind. Let me come. I hear from my previous employers that I was a damn good surgeon. I can be of use to you and the casualties."

His frown dissolved, until his smile blinded her with his delight. "This isn't how I visualized spending our wedding night, *mi corazon*. But having you across a table in my OR is second on my list only to having you wrapped all around me in my bed."

After the emergency, during which their intervention was thankfully lifesaving, they had two weeks of total seclusion on his estate.

The three weeks after that, Cybele ticked off the two top items on Rodrigo's list, over and over. Daily, in fact.

They worked together during the days, discovering yet another area in which they were attuned. It became a constant joy and stimulation, to keep realizing how fully they could share their lives and careers.

Then came the nights. And if their first time and their semi-aborted wedding night had been world-shaking, she'd had no idea how true intimacy would escalate the pleasure and creativity of their encounters. Even those momentous occasions paled by comparison.

It was their five-week anniversary today.

She was in her twenty-second week of pregnancy and she'd never felt healthier or happier. Not that that convinced Rodrigo to change her prenatal checkups from weekly to biweekly.

"Ready, *mi amor?*"

She sprang to her feet, dissolved into his embrace. He kissed her until she was wrapped around him, begging him to postpone her checkup. She had an emergency only he could handle.

He bit her lip gently, put her away. "It'll take all of fifteen minutes. Then I'm all yours. As always."

She hooked her arm through his, inhaled his hormone-stimulating scent. "Do you want to find out the gender of the baby?"

He looked at her intently, as if wanting to make sure of her wish before he voiced his opinion. Seemed he didn't want to risk volunteering one that opposed hers. "Do you?"

She decided to let the delicious man off the hook. "I do."

His smile dawned. He *did* want to know, but considered it up to her to decide. Surely she couldn't love him more, could she?

"Then we find out."

"So what do you hope it is?"

He didn't hesitate, nuzzled her neck, whispered, "A girl. A tiny replica of her unique mother."

She surrendered to his cosseting, delight swirling inside her. "Would you be disappointed if it's a boy?"

His smile answered unequivocally. "I'm just being greedy. And then, you know how seriously cool it is to be female around here."

She made the goofy gesture and expression that had become their catchphrase. "Women rule."

Four hours later, they were back in their bedroom.

They'd made love for two of those, only stopped because

they had a dinner date with Ramón and other colleagues in Barcelona.

She was leaning into him, gazing in wonder at his reflection in the mirror as he towered behind her, kissing her neck, caressing her zipper up her humming body, taking extra care of her rounding belly. She sighed her bliss. "Think Steven and Agnes will be happy it's a boy?"

His indulgent smile didn't waver. But she was so attuned to his every nuance of expression now, she could tell the question disturbed him. Since it indirectly brought up Mel.

And the mention of Mel had been the only thing to make him tense since they'd gotten married, to make him even testy and irritated. He'd once even snapped at her. She'd been shocked that day. And for a moment, black thoughts had swamped her.

She'd wondered if this fierceness was different from his early moroseness concerning Mel, if now that he was her husband, Mel was no longer simply his dead foster brother, but her dead first husband and he hated her mentioning Mel, out of jealousy.

The implications of that were so insupportable, she'd nearly choked on them. But only for a moment. Then he'd apologized so incredibly and she'd remembered what he was, what Mel had been to him.

She'd come to the conclusion that the memory of Mel was still a gaping wound inside him. One that hurt more as time passed, as the loss solidified. With him busy being the tower of strength everyone clung to, he hadn't dealt with his own grief. He hadn't attained the closure he'd made possible for everyone else to have. She hoped their baby would heal the wound, provide that closure.

His hands resumed caressing her belly. "I think they'll be happy as long as the baby is healthy."

And she had to get something else out of the way. "I called

Agnes this morning and she sounded happier than I've ever heard her. She said those who filed the lawsuits weren't creditors but investors who gave Mel money to invest in the hospital, and that the money was found in an account they didn't know about."

His hands stopped their caresses. "That's right."

"But why didn't they ask for their money instead of resorting to legal action, adding insult to injury to bereaved parents? A simple request would have sent Agnes and Steven looking through Mel's documents and talking to his lawyer and accountant."

"Maybe they feared Agnes and Steven wouldn't give back the money without a strong incentive."

"Apart from finding this an incredibly irrational fear since Mel and his parents are upstanding people, there must have been legal provisos in place to assure everyone's rights."

"I don't know why they acted as they did. What's important is that the situation's over, and no harm's done to anyone."

And she saw it in his eyes. The lie.

She grabbed his hands. "You're not telling me the truth." He tried to pull his hand away. She clung. "Please, tell me."

That bleak look, which she'd almost forgotten had ever marred his beauty, was back like a swirl of ink muddying clear water.

But it was worse. He pushed away from her, glared at her in the mirror like a tiger enraged at someone pulling on a half ripped-out claw.

"You want the truth? Or do you just want me to confirm that those people acted irrationally, that Mel was an upstanding man? If so, you should do like Agnes and Steven, grab at my explanation for this mess, turn a blind eye and cling to your illusions."

She swung around to face him. "You made up this story to

comfort them. The debts were real. And you must have done more than settle them to make Mel's creditors change their story."

"What do you care about the sordid details?"

Sordid? Oh, God. "Did…did I have something to do with this? Are you still protecting me, too?"

"*No.* You had nothing to do with any of it. It was just more lies Mel fed me, poisoned me with. I lived my life cleaning up after him, covering up for him. And now he's reaching back from the grave and forcing me to keep on doing it. And you know what? I'm *sick* of it. I've been getting sicker by the day, of embellishing his image and memory to you, to Agnes and Steven, of gritting my teeth on the need to tell you what I figured out he'd done to me. To *us.*"

She staggered backward under the impact of his exasperated aggression. "What did he do? And what do you mean, to 'us'?"

"How can I tell you? It would be my word against a man who can't defend himself. It would make me a monster in your eyes."

"No." She threw herself in his path. "Nothing would make you anything but the man I love with every fiber of my being."

He held her at arm's length. "Just forget it, Cybele. I shouldn't have said anything…*Dios,* I wish I could take it back."

But the damage had been done. Rodrigo's feelings about Mel seemed to be worse than she'd ever feared. And she had to know. The rest. Everything. Now. "Please, Rodrigo, I have to know."

"How can I begin to explain, when you don't even remember how *we* first met?"

She stared at him, the ferocity of his frustration pummeling her, bloodying her. She gasped, the wish to remember so violent, it smashed at the insides of her skull like giant hammers.

Suddenly, the last barricade shattered. Memories burst out of the last dark chasm in her mind, snowballing into an avalanche.

She remembered.

Thirteen

She swung away, a frantic beast needing a way out.

The world tilted, the ground rushed at her at a crazy angle.

"*Cybele.*"

Her name thundered over her, then lightning hit her, intercepted her fall, live wires snaring her in cabled strength before she reinjured her arm beneath her plummeting weight.

Memories flooded through her like water through a drowning woman's lungs. In brutal sequence.

She'd first seen Rodrigo at a fundraiser for her hospital. Across the ballroom, towering above everyone, canceling out their existence. She'd felt hit by lightning then, too.

She'd stood there, unable to tear her eyes off him as people kept swamping him in relentless waves, moths to his irresistible fire. All through, he'd somehow never taken his eyes off her. She'd been sure she'd seen the same response in his eyes, the same inability to believe its power, to resist it.

Then Ramón had joined him, turned to look at her, too, and she knew Rodrigo was telling him about her. He left Ramón's side, charted a course for her. She stood there, shaking, knowing her life would change the moment he reached her.

Then a man next to her had collapsed. Even disoriented by Rodrigo's hypnotic effect, her doctor auto-function took over, and she'd rushed to the man's rescue.

She'd kept up her resuscitation efforts until paramedics came, and then she'd swayed up to look frantically for Rodrigo. But he'd vanished.

Disappointment crushed her even when she kept telling herself she'd imagined it all, her own response, too, that if she'd talked to him she would have found out he was nothing like the man she'd created in her mind.

Within days, she'd met Mel. He came with a huge donation to her hospital and became the head of the new surgery department. He offered her a position and started pursuing her almost at once. Flattered by his attention, she'd accepted a couple of dates. Then he proposed. By then, she had suspected he was a risk-taking jerk, and turned him down. But he'd said he used that persona at work to keep everyone on their toes, and showed himself to be diametrically different, everything she'd hoped for in a man, until she accepted.

Then Mel had introduced Rodrigo as his best friend.

She was shocked—and distraught that she hadn't imagined his effect on her. But she'd certainly imagined her effect on him. He seemed to find her abhorrent. Mel, unaware of the tension between the two people he said meant the most to him, insisted on having Rodrigo with them all the time. And though Mel's bragging accounts of his friend's mile-high bedpost notches had her despising Rodrigo right back, she'd realized she couldn't marry Mel while she felt that unstoppable attraction to his best friend. So she broke off the engagement. And it was then that

Mel drove off in a violent huff and had the accident that had crippled him.

Feeling devastated by guilt when Mel accused her of being the reason he'd been crippled, Cybele took back her ring. They got married in a ceremony attended by only his parents a month after he was discharged from hospital. Rodrigo had left for Spain after he'd made sure there was nothing more he could do for his friend at that time, and to Cybele's relief, he didn't attend.

But the best of intentions didn't help her cope with the reality of living with a bitter, volatile man. They'd discussed with a specialist the ways to have a sex life, but his difficulties had agonized him even though Cybele assured him it didn't matter. She didn't feel the loss of what she'd never had, was relieved when Mel gave up trying, and poured her energy into helping him return to the OR while struggling to catch up with her job.

Then Rodrigo came back, and Mel's erratic behavior spiked. She'd confronted him, and he said he felt insecure around any able-bodied man, especially Rodrigo, but needed him more than ever. He was the world's leading miracle worker in spinal injuries, and he was working on putting Mel back on his feet.

But there was one thing Mel needed even more now. He was making progress with the sex therapy specialists, but until he could be a full husband to her, he wanted something to bind them, beyond her sense of duty and honor and a shared house. A baby.

Cybele had known he was testing her commitment. But was feeling guiltier now that she'd lived with his affliction reason enough to take such a major step at such an inappropriate time? Would a baby make him feel more of a man? Was it wise to introduce a baby into the instability of their relationship?

Guilt won, and with her mother promising she'd help out with the baby, she had the artificial insemination.

Within a week, her conception was confirmed. The news only made Mel unbearably volatile, until she'd said she was done tiptoeing around him since it only made him worse. He apologized, said he couldn't take the pressure, needed time off. And again Cybele succumbed, suspended her residency even knowing she'd lose her position, to help him and to work out their problems. Then he dropped another bombshell on her. He wanted them to spend that time off on Rodrigo's estate.

When she'd resisted, he said it would be a double benefit, as Rodrigo wanted Mel there for tests for the surgeries that would give Mel back the use of his legs. And she'd had to agree.

When they'd arrived in Barcelona, Rodrigo had sent them a limo. Mel had it drive them to the airfield where his plane was kept. When she objected, he said he didn't need legs to fly, that flying would make him feel like he was whole again.

But during the flight, in answer to some innocuous comments, he got nasty then abusive. She held her tongue and temper, knowing it wasn't the place to escalate their arguments, but she decided that once they landed, she'd face him, as she'd faced herself, and say that their relationship wasn't working, and it wasn't because of his turmoil, but because of who he was. A man of a dual nature, one side she'd loved but could no longer find, and the other she couldn't bear and seemed was all that remained.

But they hadn't landed.

Now she heaved as the collage of the crash detonated in image after shearing image, accompanied by a hurricane of deafening cacophony and suffocating terror.

Then the maelstrom exchanged its churning motion for a linear trajectory as all trivial memories of every day of the year before the accident burst like flashes of sickening light, obliterating the blessed darkness of the past months.

Everything decelerated, came to a lurching stop.

Her face was being wiped in coolness, her whole self bathed in Rodrigo's concern. She raised sore eyes to his reddened ones.

His lips feathered over them with trembling kisses. "You remember."

"My end of things," she rasped. "Tell me yours."

The heart beneath her ear felt as if it would ram out of his chest.

Then he spoke. "When I saw you at that fundraiser, it was like seeing my destiny. I told Ramón that, and he said that if anyone else had said that, he would have laughed. But coming from me, I, who always know what's right for me, he believed it, and to go get you. But as I moved to do that, all hell broke loose. You rushed to that man's aid and I was called to deal with multiple neuro-trauma cases back here. I asked Ramón to find out all he could about you, so I could seek you out the moment I came back.

"I tried for the last almost eighteen months not to reconstruct what I instinctively knew and didn't want to—*couldn't* face. But the more I knew you, the more inconsistencies I discovered since the accident, the more I couldn't pretend not to know how it all happened anymore. Mel was there, too, that initial day. He was right behind me as I turned away from Ramón. He must have overheard my intentions. And he decided to beat me to you."

She couldn't even gasp. Shock fizzled inside her like a spark in a depleted battery.

"And he did. Using money I gave him to gain his new position, he put himself where he'd have access to you. For the six weeks I stayed away performing one surgery after another, all the time burning for the moment I could come back and search you out, he was pursuing you. The moment you accepted his proposal, he called me to tell me that he was engaged. He left your name out.

"The day I rushed back to the States to find you, he insisted I go see him first, meet his fiancée. I can never describe my horror when I found out it was you.

"I kept telling myself it couldn't have been intentional, that he wouldn't be so cruel, that he couldn't be shoving down my throat the fact that he was the one who'd gotten you. But I remember his glee as he recounted how it had been love at first sight, that you couldn't get enough of him, and realized he was having a huge laugh at my expense, wallowing in his triumph over me, all the while dangling you in front of me until I was crazed with pain."

"Was that why…?" She choked off. It was too much.

"Why I behaved as if I hated you? *Sí.* I hated everything at the time. Mel, myself, you, the world, the very life I woke up to every morning in which you could never be mine."

"B-but you had so many other lovers."

"I had *nobody*. Since I laid eyes on you. Those women were smoke screens so that I wouldn't sit through our outings like a third-wheel fool, something to distract me so I wouldn't lose my mind wanting you more with each passing day. But nothing worked. Not my efforts to despise you, not your answering antipathy. So I left, and would have never come back. But he forced me back. He crippled himself, as I and his parents always warned him he one day would."

A shudder rattled her at the memory. "He said I made him lose his mind, drove him to it…."

He looked beyond horrified. "*No. Dios,* Cybele…it had *nothing* to do with you, do you hear? Mel never took responsibility for any problem he created for himself. He always found someone else to accuse, usually me or his parents. *Dios*—that he turned on you, too, accused you of this!" His face turned a burnt bronze, his lips worked, thinning with the effort to contain his aggression. She had the feeling that if Mel were alive and here, Rodrigo would have dragged him out of his wheelchair and taken him apart.

At last he rasped, "It had to do with his own gambler's behavior. He always took insane risks, in driving, in sports, in surgeries. One of those insane risks was the gambling that landed him in so much debt. I gave him the money to gamble, too. He told me it was to buy you the things you wanted. But I investigated. He never bought you anything."

So this was it. The explanation he'd withheld.

"As for the stunt that cost him his life and could have cost yours, it wasn't his first plane crash but his third. He walked away from so many disasters he caused without a scratch that even the one that cut him in half didn't convince him that his luck had run out and the next time would probably be fatal. As it was."

For a long moment, all she heard was her choppy breath, the blood swooshing in her ears, his harsh breathing.

Then he added, "Or maybe he wanted to die."

"Why would he?" she rasped. "He believed you'd put him back on his feet. He said you were very optimistic."

He looked as if he'd explode. "Then he lied to you. Again. There was nothing I could do for him. I made it absolutely clear."

She squeezed her eyes shut. "So he was really desperate."

"I think he was worse than that." His hiss felt as if it would scrape her flesh from her bone. "I think he'd gone over the edge, wanted to take you with him. So I would never have you."

She lurched as if under a flesh-gouging lash.

Rodrigo went on, bitterness pouring out of him. "Mel

always had a sickness. Me. Since the first day I set foot in the Braddocks' house, he idolized me and seethed with jealousy of me, alternated between emulating me to the point of impersonation, to doing everything to be my opposite, between loving and hating me."

It all made so much sense it was horrifying. How she'd found Mel so different at first, how he'd switched to the seamless act of emulating Rodrigo. So it *had* been Rodrigo she'd fallen in love with all along. It was unbelievable. Yet it was the truth.

And it dictated her next action. The only thing she could do.

She pushed out of his arms, rose to unsteady feet, looked down at him, the man she loved beyond life itself.

And she cut her heart out. "I want a divorce."

Cybele's demand fell on Rodrigo like a scythe.

Rage, at himself, hacked him much more viciously.

He'd been so *stupid*. He'd railed at a dead man, not just the man he'd considered his younger brother, but the man Cybele still loved, evidently more than she could ever love him.

He shot to his feet, desperation the one thing powering him. "Cybele, *no. Lo siento, mi amor.* I didn't mean…"

She shut her eyes in rejection, stopping his apology and explanation. "You meant every word. And you had every right. Because you *are* right. You at last explained my disappointment in Mel, my resentment toward him. You rid me of any guilt I ever felt toward him."

Rodrigo reeled. "You—you didn't love Mel?"

She shook her head. Then in a dead monotone, she told him her side of the story.

"Seems I always sensed his manipulations, even if I would have never guessed their reason or extent. My subconscious must have considered it a violation, so it wiped out the traumatic time until I was strong enough. I still woke up with overpowering gut feelings. But without context, they weren't enough to stop me from tormenting myself when I felt nothing but relief at his death and anger toward him, when I wanted you from the moment I woke up. Now I know. I always wanted you."

Elation and confusion tore him in two. "You did? *Dios*—then why are you asking for a divorce?"

"Because I don't matter. Only my baby does. I would never have married you if I'd realized you would be the worst father for him. Instead of loving his father, you hate Mel with a lifelong passion. And though you have every right to feel that way, I can never subject my child to the life I had. Worse than the life I had. My stepfather didn't know my father, and he also didn't consider me the bane of his life. He just cared nothing for me. But it was my mother's love for him, her love for the children she had with him, that alienated her from me. And she doesn't love him a fraction of how much I love you."

He should have realized all that. He knew her scars in detail, knew she was barely coping now, as an adult, with her alienated childhood and current bland family situation. But he got it now. The sheer magnitude of his blunder. It could cost him his life. *Her.*

"I never hated Mel," he pleaded. "It was Mel who considered me the usurper of his parents' respect and affection. I loved him, like brothers love their imperfect siblings. Mel did have a lot to him that I appreciated, and I always hoped he'd believe that, be happy playing on his own strengths and stop competing with me in mine. But I could never convince him, and it ate at him until he lashed out, injured you while trying to get to me, the source of his discontent. It was foolish, tragic, and I *do* hate his taking you away from me, but I don't hate *him*. You have to believe that."

She clearly didn't. And she had every reason to distrust his words after that moronic display of bitterness and anger.

She confirmed his worst fears, her voice as inanimate as her face. "I can't take the chance with my baby's life."

Agony bled out of him. "Do you think so little of me, Cybele? You claim to love me, and you still think I'd be so petty, so cruel, as to take whatever I felt for Mel out on an innocent child?"

She stumbled two steps back to escape his pleading hands. "You might not be able to help it. He did injure you, repeatedly, throughout his life. That he's now dead doesn't mean that you can forget. Or forgive. I wouldn't blame you if you could do neither."

"But that baby is *yours*, Cybele. He could be yours from the very devil and I'd still love and cherish him because he's yours. Because I love you. I would die for you."

The stone that seemed to be encasing her cracked, and she came apart, a mass of tremors and tears. "And I would d-die for you. I feel I *will* die without you. And that only makes me more scared, of what I'd do to please you, to keep your love, if I weaken now, and it turns out, with your best intentions, you'd never be able to love my baby as he deserves to be loved. And I—I can't risk that. Please, I beg you, don't make it impossible to leave you. *Please*…let me go."

He lunged for her, as if to grab her before she vanished. "I *can't*, Cybele."

She wrenched away, tears splashing over his hands. His arms fell to his sides, empty, pain impaling his heart, despair wrecking his sanity.

Suddenly, realization hit him like a vicious uppercut.

He couldn't *believe* it. *Dios*, he was far worse than a moron.

He *did* have the solution to everything.

He blocked her path. "*Querida*, forgive me, I'm such an idiot. I conditioned myself so hard to never let the truth slip, that even after you told me your real feelings for Mel, it took seeing you almost walking out on me to make me realize I don't have to hide it anymore. It is true I would have loved any baby of yours as mine, no matter what. But I love *this* baby, I want him and I would die for him, too. Because he *is* mine. Literally."

Fourteen

"I *am* the baby's father."

Cybele stared at Rodrigo, comprehension suspended.

"If you don't believe me, a DNA test will prove it."

And it ripped through her like a knife in her gut.

One thing was left in her mind, in the world. A question.

She croaked it. "How?"

He looked as if he'd rather she asked him to step in front of a raging bull. Then he exhaled. "A few years back, Mel had a paternity suit. During the tests to prove that he didn't father the child, he found out that he was infertile. Then he told me that you were demanding proof of his commitment to your marriage, the emotional security of a baby. He said he couldn't bear to reveal another shortcoming to you, that he couldn't lose you, that you were what kept him alive. He asked me to donate the sperm. Just imagining you blossoming with my baby, nurturing it, while I could never claim it or you, almost killed *me*.

"But I believed him when he said he'd die if you left him. And even suspecting how he'd stolen you from me, I would have done anything to save him. And I knew if I said no, he would have gotten any sperm donor sample and passed it as his. I couldn't have you bear some stranger's baby. So I agreed.

"But believing you were suffering from psychogenic amnesia so that your mind wouldn't buckle under the trauma of losing him, I couldn't let you know you'd lost what you thought remained of him. I wouldn't cause you further psychological damage. I would have settled for being my baby's father by adoption when he was mine for real."

So that was why. His change toward her after the accident, treating her like she was the most precious thing in the world, binding himself to her forever. This explained everything much more convincingly than his claim that he'd loved her all along.

It had all been for his baby.

"Te quiero tanto, Cybele, *más que la vida. Usted es mi corazón, mi alma."*

Hearing him say he loved her, more than life, that she was his heart, his soul now that she knew the truth was…unbearable.

Feeling her life had come to an end, she pushed out of his arms and ran.

Rodrigo restrained himself from charging after her and hauling her back and never letting her go ever again with an exertion of will that left him panting.

He had to let her go. She had to have time alone to come to terms with the shocks, to realize that although they'd taken a rough course to reach this point, both Mel and fate had ended up giving them their future and perfect happiness together.

He lasted an hour. Then he went after her. He found her gone.

Consuelo told him Cybele had asked Gustavo to drive her to the city, where he'd dropped her off at a hotel near the center.

He felt as if the world had vanished from around him.

She'd left him. But…why? She'd said she loved him, too.

When his head was almost bursting with confusion and dread, he found a note on their bed.

The lines swam as if under a lens of trembling liquid.

> *Rodrigo,*
> *You should have told me that my baby was yours from the start. I would have accepted your care for its real reason—a man safeguarding the woman who is carrying his baby. Knowing you and your devotion to family, your need to have your flesh and blood surrounding you, I know you want this baby fiercely, want to give him the most stable family you can, the one neither of us had. Had you told me, I would have done anything to cooperate with you so the baby would have parents who dote on him and who treat each other with utmost affection and respect. I don't have to be your wife to do that. You can divorce me if you wish, and I'll still remain your friend and colleague, will live in Spain as long as you do, so you'll have constant access to your son.*
> *Cybele.*

Rodrigo read the note until he felt the words begin to burn a brand into his retinas, his brain.

After all the lies and manipulations she'd been victim to, she had every right to distrust his emotions and motives toward her. From her standpoint, he could be saying and doing whatever it took to get his son.

But he'd prove his sincerity if it was the last thing he did.

If he lost her, it just might be.

Twenty-four hours later, he stood outside her hotel room door, feeling he'd aged twenty-four years.

She opened the door, looking as miserable as he felt.

All he wanted was to take her in his arms, kiss her until she was incoherent with desire, but he knew that might only prove to her that he was manipulating her even worse than Mel had.

He never gambled. But he'd never known true desperation, either. Now a gamble, with potentially catastrophic results, was the last resort he had left.

Without a word, he handed her the divorce papers.

Cybele's heart stopped, felt it would never beat again.

She'd made a desperate gamble. And lost. She'd owed him the choice, the freedom to have his baby without remaining her husband. She'd prayed he'd choose to be with her anyway.

He hadn't. He was giving her proof, now that she'd assured him he'd always have his son, that he'd rather be free of her.

Then her eyes fell on the heading of one of the papers.

Before the dread fully formed inside her mind, it spilled from her lips. "You won't take the baby away, will you? Any court in the world would give you custody, I know, but please don't—"

He grimaced as if she'd stabbed him. "Cybele, *querida, por favor, le pido.* I beg you…stop. Do you distrust me that much?"

Mortification swallowed her whole. "No…no—oh, God. But I—I don't *know.* Anything. It's like you're three people in my mind. The one who seemed to hate me, the one who saved me, took such infinite care of me, who seemed to want me as much as I want you, and the one who always had an agenda, who's handing me divorce papers. I don't know who you are, or what to believe anymore."

"Let me explain." His hands descended on her shoulders.

"No." She staggered around before his grip could tighten. She couldn't hear that he cared, but not enough to remain married to her. She fumbled for a pen by the hotel's writing pad. The papers slid from her hands, scattered across the desk. Fat tears splashed over the blurring lines that mimicked the chaos inside her. "After I sign these papers, I want a couple of days. I'll call you when I'm thinking straight again and we can discuss how we handle things from now on."

His hands clamped the top of her arms, hauled her back against the living rock of his body. She struggled to escape, couldn't bear the agony his feel, his touch, had coursing in hers.

He pressed her harder to his length. She felt his hardness digging into her buttocks, couldn't understand.

He still wanted her? But if he was divorcing her, then all the hunger she'd thought only she could arouse in him had just been the insatiable sexual appetite of the hot-blooded male that he was. And now…what? Her struggles were arousing him?

All thought evaporated as his lips latched onto her neck, drew on her flesh, wrenching her desire, her very life force with openmouthed kisses and suckles. She tried to twist away, but he lifted her off the ground, carried her to the wall, spread her against it and pinned her there with his bulk, his knee driven between her thighs, his erection grinding against her belly.

He caught her lower lip in a growling bite, sucked and pulled on it until she cried out, opened wide for him. Then he plunged, took, gave, tongue and teeth and voracity. Wave after wave of readiness flooded her core. She squirmed against him, everything disintegrating with her need to crawl under his skin, take him into hers. His fingers found her under her panties, probed her to a screeching climax. Then she begged for him.

In a few moments and moves, he gave her more than she could take, all of him, driving inside her drenched, clenching tightness. Pleasure detonated from every inch of flesh that yielded to the invasion of the red-hot satin of his thickness and length. He powered into her, poured driven words in an inextricable mix of English and Catalan, of love and lust and unbearable pleasure into her gasping mouth as his thrusting tongue ravaged her with possession and mindlessness.

Pleasure reverberated inside her with each thrust, each word, each melding kiss, like the rushing and receding of a tide gone mad. It all gathered, towered, held at its zenith like a tidal wave before the devastating crash. Then the blows of release hit like those of a giant hammer, striking her core again and again, expanding shock waves that razed her, wrung her around his girth in contractions so violent they fractured breath and heartbeats. She clung to him in the frenzy, inside and out as if she'd assimilate him, dissolve around him. Then she felt him roar his release as he jammed his erection to her womb, jetting his pleasure to fill it, causing another wave to crash over her, shattering her with the power of the sensations, of wishing that they'd make a baby this way in the future. When they didn't have one…

She came back to awareness to find him beneath her on the bed, still hard and pulsating inside her, setting off mini quakes that kept her in a state of continuous orgasm.

A question wavered from her in a scratchy rasp. "So was that goodbye sex?"

He jerked beneath her. "You go out of your way to pick the exact words that will cut me deepest, don't you?"

And she wailed, "What else could it be?"

"It was you-turn-me-into-a-raging-beast-in-perpetual-mating-frenzy sex. It was I-can't-have-enough-of-your-pleasure-and-your-intimacy lovemaking." Every word flowed over her like a balm on a wound, drowning the doubt demons who whispered he was just over-endowed and would enjoy any sexually voracious female. "Not that that excuses what I did. I didn't come here intending to take you like that. I was resolved not to confuse issues. But I saw you about to sign those papers and almost burst an artery."

Her lips twitched in spite of her confusion. "Glad the pressure found another outlet." She relived the moments when it had, splashing against her inner walls, filling her with his scalding essence, mixing with her pleasure... But...wait a sec! "But you *want* me to sign the papers."

He rose onto his elbow, looked at her with the last trace of heavy-lidded male possession vanishing, that bleakness taking over his eyes. "I want a bullet between the eyes more." She gasped, the thought of anything happening to him paralyzing her with terror. "But since I can't prove that to you by words or lovemaking, and you have every right not to accept either as proof, after all the lies that almost cost you your mind and your very life, I'm down to action. And the proof of time."

He extricated himself from her, rose off the bed, walked to gather the papers and came back to lay them beside her.

Before she could say she didn't want any proof, just wanted to be his, if he really wanted her, he turned and gathered his clothes.

She sat up shakily as he started dressing, his movements stiff, his face clenched with that intensity she now believed betrayed his turmoil. And finally, she understood. Just as she'd given him the freedom to divorce her, the divorce papers were his proof that she was equally free. Even if he'd rather end his life than lose her, he was letting her go, if it meant her peace of mind. Oh, God...

She'd caused him so much pain, even if inadvertently. Then, when he'd told her how long and how much he'd been hurting, she'd added indelible insult to injury when she'd imposed her distrust of those who'd blighted her life with letdowns, who'd made her doubt that she was deserving of love, as pretext to condemn his motivations.

But a man who wanted only his child wouldn't have done one thousandth of the things he'd done for her. He would never have said he loved her, would rather die than lose her. And even if any other man might have lied to that extent to achieve what he considered a highest cause, the stability of his child's family life, Rodrigo wouldn't. He was too honorable.

Even when he'd kept the truth about their baby's paternity from her, he'd done it only to protect her, had been willing to never proclaim his baby as his own flesh and blood, to preserve the illusion he'd thought essential to her well-being.

She made a grab for the papers, sprang off the bed and ran to him, grabbed one of his hands as he started buttoning up his shirt, tears of humility and contrition and heart-piercing adoration pouring from her very soul to scorch down her cheeks. "Those papers are your I'm-free-to-come-back-to-you-of-my-own-free-will gesture, right?"

He seemed to struggle to stop himself. He lost the fight, reached out with his other hand, wiped away her tears, cupped her cheek, his face the embodiment of tenderness. "They're not a gesture. You *are* free. And you must not consider me in your decision. You're not responsible for how I feel." Exactly the opposite of what Mel and her family had done to her. They'd made her feel responsible for their feelings toward her, guilty of inciting Mel's pathological possessiveness or their equally unnatural negligence. "In time, if you become satisfied that I am what you need, what will make you happy, come back to me. If you don't, then sign those papers and send them back to me instead. The other documents should prove you are in no way pressured to make the best of it for anybody else's sake but yours."

And she revealed her last and biggest fear. "W-what if in time *you* decide I'm not what you need?"

He huffed a harsh laugh, as if she were asking if he might one day fly under his own power. Certainty solidified in her every cell as she grinned up at him with sudden unbridled ecstasy. Then the rest of his words registered. "The other documents…"

She looked through the papers, found those with the heading that had triggered her crazy doubt that he'd take the baby.

Custody papers. Giving away his parental rights. To her. Unconditionally. She'd choose if he was part of his baby's life.

She stared at the words, their meaning too huge to take in.

Her eyes flew dazedly up to his solemn ones. "Why?"

"Because without you, nothing is worth having, not even my child. Because I trust you not to deprive him of my love even if you decide to end our marriage. Because I want you to be totally free to make that decision if you need to, without fearing you'll lose your baby, or become embroiled in a custody case. Because I need to know that if you come back to me, you do it not out of need or gratitude or for our baby's best interests, but because it's in *your* best interests. Because you want me."

Then he turned away, looking like a man who had nothing to look forward to but waiting for an uncertain verdict.

She flew after him, joy and distress tearing at her. She wrenched him around, jumped on him, climbed him, wrapped herself around him and squeezed him as if she'd merge them. His shuddering groan quaked through her as he hugged her back, crushed her to him, his arms trembling his relief.

She covered his face and neck and anything she could reach

of him in tear-drenched kisses and wept. "I don't just *want* you! I worship you, I crave and adore and love you far more than life. And it's not out of need or gratitude. Not the way you fear. I don't need you to survive, but I need you to be alive. I'm grateful you exist, and a few light years beyond that that you love me, too. I don't deserve you or that you should feel the same for me. I—I hurt you and mistrusted you and it doesn't matter that I was reeling from the shock of the regained memories and the revelations—"

His lips crushed the rest of her outburst in savage kisses. Then she was on the bed again, on her back, filled with him as he drove into her, growled to her again and again that he believed her and in her, and she screamed and sobbed her relief and gratitude and love and pleasure.

It was hours before that storm abated and she lay over him, free of doubt or worry, of gravity and physical limitations.

She told him, "You make me feel—limitless, just like what I feel for you. But you are too much, give too much. It would have been criminal to have all this without paying in advance with some serious misery and heartache. I love the fates that tossed me around only to land me in your lap, and by some miracle make you love me, too. I just adore every bit of misfortune and unhappiness I had that now make me savor every second of what we share all the more."

Rodrigo swept Cybele with caresses, agreed to every word she said. They were the exact ones that filled his being. He did believe they wouldn't have come to share this purity and intensity without surviving so many tests and...

He shot up, his nerves going haywire.

Under his palm. He'd felt it.

"The baby..." he choked. "He moved." And for the first time

since he'd shed tears over his mother's death, his tears flowed. With too much love, pride and gratitude.

She pushed him onto his back, rained frantic kisses all over his face. "No, please—I can't bear seeing your tears, even ones of joy." That only made the tears flow thicker. After moments of panting consternation, wickedness replaced the stricken look on her face and she attacked him with tickling.

He guffawed and flopped her onto her back, imprisoning what he swore were electricity- and magic-wielding hands over her head with one of his, his other returning the sensual torment.

She squirmed under his hand, nuzzled his chest. "I can't wait to have our baby. And I can't wait to have another one. One we'll make as we lose ourselves in love and pleasure, flesh in flesh."

"This one *was* made of our love…well, my love, at least."

She nipped him. "Yeah, I have to make up for my initial lack of participation in the love department. But from now on, I'm sharing everything with you. And not only about our baby. I want to be involved in everything you do, your research, your surgeries…." The radiant animation on her face faltered. "Uh—that came out as if I'll hound your every step…."

He squeezed her, cutting short her mortification, laughter booming out of his depths. "Oh, please, do. Gives me an excuse to hound yours." Then he grew serious. "But I know exactly how you meant it. I want you involved in everything I do, too. I've never felt more stimulated, more empowered, more satisfied with my work than when you were there with me. And then there's every other instance when I see or feel or think anything, and it isn't right, isn't complete until I share it with you, knowing you're the only one who'll understand, appreciate."

She attacked him with another giggling, weeping kiss

that almost extracted his soul. Then she raised a radiant face, gestured for him to stay where he was.

He watched her bounce out of bed to rummage in her suitcase. He hardened to steel again, licking at the lingering taste of her on his lips as she walked back, ripe and tousled and a little awkward, all the effects of his love and loving, short- and long-term ones. She was holding something behind her back, impishness turning her beauty from breathtaking to heartbreaking.

"Close your eyes." He chuckled, obeyed at once. He couldn't wait to "see" what she had in store for him.

Her weight dipped the mattress. Then he almost came off it.

She was licking him. All over his chest and abdomen.

He growled, tried to hold her head closer, thrusting at her, offering all of him for her delicate devouring.

"Keep those lethal weapons of yours closed."

He did, his heart almost rattling the whole bed in anticipation. Then he felt a sting on his chest.

The tail end of the sensation was a lance of pleasure that corkscrewed to his erection. It slammed against his abdomen. Air left his lungs on a bellow of stimulation.

Another sting followed. Then another and another, on a path of fiery pain and pleasure down his body. He'd never felt anything like this sourceless manipulation of his sensations. He could swear she wasn't touching him, was pricking each individual nerve cluster mentally.

He thrust at her, incoherent with arousal, his growls becoming those of a beast in a frenzy. He at last thrust his hands into her hair, tugged until she moaned with enjoyment.

"Tell me to open my eyes," he panted the order, the plea.

Another skewer of delight. "Uh-uh."

"I don't need them open to take you until you weep with

pleasure," he threatened, almost weeping himself again with the sharpness of the sensations she'd buried him under.

"Which you routinely do." Another sting. He roared. She purred, "Okay, just because you threatened so nicely. Open 'em."

He did. And couldn't credit their evidence for moments.

Then he rasped between gasps as she continued her meticulous sensual torture, "This is—hands down—the most innovative use of a micro-grasping forceps I've ever seen."

She was tugging at his hairs using the most delicate forceps used in micro-neurosurgery. And sending him stark raving mad.

"It's also the most hands-on method I could think of to say thanks." Her eyes glittered up at him, flooding him with love.

"Not that I'm not deliriously thankful for whatever made you invent this new…procedure, but thanks for what, *mi vida?*"

"Thanks for all the patience and perseverance you put into getting my hand back to this level of fine coordination."

He dropped his gaze to her hand. It was true. There was no sign of clumsiness, weakness or pain as her precious hand performed her pioneering form of carnal torment.

He groaned, glided her over his aching body, grasped her hand gently and took it to his lips, thanked the fates for her, for letting him be the instrument of her happiness and well-being.

"Thank *you*, for existing, for letting me be forever yours."

Cybele cupped his face as he continued his homage, wondering how one being could contain all the love she felt for him.

She caressed his hewn cheek, traced the planes of his chiseled lips. "If you're satisfied with my precision, can I apprentice at your hands in neurosurgery?"

He enfolded her and she felt as if his heart gave her the answer. To everything. "Just wish for it and it's done, *mi alma*. Anything you want, the whole world is yours for the asking."

She took his lips with a whimper, then she whispered into his mouth, "I already have the whole world. You, our baby and our love."

* * * * *

Harlequin Intrigue top author Delores Fossen presents
a brand-new series of breathtaking romantic suspense!
TEXAS MATERNITY: HOSTAGES
The first installment available May 2010:
THE BABY'S GUARDIAN

Shaw cursed and hooked his arm around Sabrina.

Despite the urgency that the deadly gunfire created, he tried to be careful with her, and he took the brunt of the fall when he pulled her to the ground. His shoulder hit hard, but he held on tight to his gun so that it wouldn't be jarred from his hand.

Shaw didn't stop there. He crawled over Sabrina, sheltering her pregnant belly with his body, and he came up ready to return fire.

This was obviously a situation he'd wanted to avoid at all cost. He didn't want his baby in the middle of a fight with these armed fugitives, but when they fired that shot, they'd left him no choice. Now, the trick was to get Sabrina safely out of there.

"Get down," someone on the SWAT team yelled from the roof of the adjacent building.

Shaw did. He dropped lower, covering Sabrina as best he could.

There was another shot, but this one came from a rifleman on the SWAT team. Shaw didn't look up, but he heard the sound of glass being blown apart.

The shots continued, all coming from his men, which meant it might be time to try to get Sabrina to better cover. Shaw glanced at the front of the building.

So that Sabrina's pregnant belly wouldn't be smashed against the ground, Shaw eased off her and moved her to a sitting position so that her back was against the brick wall. They were close. Too close. And face-to-face.

He found himself staring right into those sea-green eyes.

How will Shaw get Sabrina out?
Follow the daring rescue and the heartbreaking
aftermath in THE BABY'S GUARDIAN by Delores Fossen,
available May 2010 from Harlequin Intrigue.

HARLEQUIN *Presents*

Bestselling Harlequin Presents® author

Lynne Graham

introduces

VIRGIN ON HER WEDDING NIGHT

Valente Lorenzatto never forgave Caroline Hales's abandonment of him at the altar. But now he's made millions and claimed his aristocratic Venetian birthright—and he's poised to get his revenge. He'll ruin Caroline's family by buying out their company and throwing them out of their mansion... unless she agrees to give him the wedding night she denied him five years ago....

**Available May 2010
from Harlequin Presents!**

HP12915

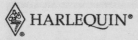

LAURA MARIE ALTOM

The Baby Twins

Stephanie Olmstead has her hands full raising
her twin baby girls on her own. When she runs
into old friend Brady Flynn, she's shocked to find
herself suddenly attracted to the handsome airline
pilot! Will this flyboy be the perfect daddy—
or will he crash and burn?

"LOVE, HOME & HAPPINESS"

www.eHarlequin.com

HAR75309

Love Inspired

Former bad boy Sloan Hawkins is back in Redemption, Oklahoma, to help keep his aunt's cherished garden thriving and to reconnect with the girl he left behind, Annie Markham. But when he discovers his secret child—and that single mother Annie never stopped loving him—he's determined that a wedding will take place in the garden nurtured by faith and love.

REDEMPTION RIVER

Where healing flows...

Look for

The Wedding Garden

by Linda Goodnight

*Available May 2010
wherever you buy books.*

Steeple
Hill®

LI87595

www.SteepleHill.com

HARLEQUIN
Ambassadors

Want to share your passion for reading Harlequin® Books?

Become a Harlequin Ambassador!

Harlequin Ambassadors are a group of passionate and well-connected readers who are willing to share their joy of reading Harlequin® books with family and friends.

You'll be sent all the tools you need to spark great conversation, including free books!

All we ask is that you share the romance with your friends and family!

You'll also be invited to have a say in new book ideas and exchange opinions with women just like you!

To see if you qualify* to be a Harlequin Ambassador, please visit www.HarlequinAmbassadors.com.

*Please note that not everyone who applies to be a Harlequin Ambassador will qualify. For more information please visit www.HarlequinAmbassadors.com.

Thank you for your participation.

BAP09BPA

REQUEST YOUR FREE BOOKS!

2 FREE NOVELS
PLUS 2
FREE GIFTS!

Silhouette

Desire

Passionate, Powerful, Provocative!

YES! Please send me 2 FREE Silhouette Desire® novels and my 2 FREE gifts (gifts are worth about $10). After receiving them, if I don't wish to receive any more books, I can return the shipping statement marked "cancel." If I don't cancel, I will receive 6 brand-new novels every month and be billed just $4.05 per book in the U.S. or $4.74 per book in Canada. That's a saving of at least 15% off the cover price! It's quite a bargain! Shipping and handling is just 50¢ per book.* I understand that accepting the 2 free books and gifts places me under no obligation to buy anything. I can always return a shipment and cancel at any time. Even if I never buy another book, the two free books and gifts are mine to keep forever.

225/326 SDN E5QG

Name _____ (PLEASE PRINT)

Address _____ Apt. #

City _____ State/Prov. _____ Zip/Postal Code

Signature (if under 18, a parent or guardian must sign)

Mail to the **Silhouette Reader Service:**

IN U.S.A.: P.O. Box 1867, Buffalo, NY 14240-1867
IN CANADA: P.O. Box 609, Fort Erie, Ontario L2A 5X3

Not valid for current subscribers to Silhouette Desire books.

Want to try two free books from another line?
Call 1-800-873-8635 or visit www.morefreebooks.com.

* Terms and prices subject to change without notice. Prices do not include applicable taxes. N.Y. residents add applicable sales tax. Canadian residents will be charged applicable provincial taxes and GST. Offer not valid in Quebec. This offer is limited to one order per household. All orders subject to approval. Credit or debit balances in a customer's account(s) may be offset by any other outstanding balance owed by or to the customer. Please allow 4 to 6 weeks for delivery. Offer available while quantities last.

Your Privacy: Silhouette Books is committed to protecting your privacy. Our Privacy Policy is available online at www.eHarlequin.com or upon request from the Reader Service. From time to time we make our lists of customers available to reputable third parties who may have a product or service of interest to you. If you would prefer we not share your name and address, please check here. ☐

Help us get it right—We strive for accurate, respectful and relevant communications. To clarify or modify your communication preferences, visit us at www.ReaderService.com/consumerchoice.

HARLEQUIN® *Blaze*™

is proud to present

New York Times bestselling author

Vicki Lewis Thompson

with a brand-new trilogy,
SONS OF CHANCE
where three sexy brothers
meet three irresistible women.

Look for the first book
WANTED!

*Available beginning in June 2010
wherever books are sold.*

---

red-hot reads

www.eHarlequin.com

HB79548